SCOTTISH ROGUES OF THE HIGH SEAS

BOUNTIES,
BEAUTIES,
&ROGUES

A strong-willed woman. A ruthless pirate. Their formidable bond.

Seonag Ruane never believed her father died in an ambush. She knows he was betrayed by men he trusted. Driven by her mother's grief and her own need for vengeance, Seonag will do whatever it takes to discover the truth. Even risk her own life. Her plan for revenge never included falling in love with the sweet-tongued pirate who shared his secrets late at night.

Captain Colin Harris's closest friend was killed by his mutinous crew. He vows to avenge his fellow pirate's death by seeking retribution and recovering the bounty the ship was transporting. It's the least he can do for the family left behind. His mission is compromised when he discovers the lad he recently hired is actually a woman in disguise and their mutual bond of trust is broken. Angered by her deceit, he imprisons the masquerader.

Seonag is certain she's failed in her quest to destroy those responsible for her father's death. How will she forgive the one man she thought she could trust? Unable to dismiss the powerful pull of attraction toward the lass, Colin decides to free her, only to learn too late that she has been captured.

Worse, he discovers that she is his late friend's daughter. Will he get to her before his mistake takes away the one woman that might make him whole?

A PIRATE'S WRATH

BRENNA ASH

Hi Liz,
Agh! Happy Sailing!
Brenna

A Pirate's Wrath
Brenna Ash

Copyright © 2021 by Brenna Ash
Dark Moor Media, LLC

Cover Design: Dar Albert, Wicked Smart Designs

Editor: Erica Monroe, Quillfire Author Services

ISBN: 978-1-955677-03-5

~

To my SSCG's. You know who you are. This book wouldn't have come together without you. A thousand thanks!

~

CHAPTER 1

Lunan Bay, Scotland
1485

*T*he days were getting longer. The crispness of the winter air was slowly being replaced with sunny, spring days. Though the temperature was still cool, the sun's rays filtering through the clouds warmed Seonag Ruane's skin as she bathed in the light.

She stood at the shoreline, and, in her mind's eye, she saw her father, Sean, at the helm of his ship, the *Revenge of Hades*. He waved to her and her mother, Margaret, as he set sail once more. Months passed each time before she saw him again.

She missed her father so. She remembered each time Sean returned. His hand filled with a new bauble of some sort. Small treasures she cherished, but none held as much value as their time spent together. A pirate's life was tough.

But even more so on the family left behind—burdening them with the constant worry and anxiety that they may never see their loved one again.

Her father had been strong. Seonag had never feared that he wouldn't return home. How stupid and naive she'd been when she was but a wee lass.

The waves were gaining height as they made their way to shore, growing in frequency, pushed by the incoming tide.

She would never forget the day the *Revenge of Hades* returned with a new captain at the helm.

Seonag remembered the crew telling her and her mother that they had been stalked and attacked by Spanish pirates. Being the brutal lot that they were, the Spaniards had killed her father. She had stood still as stone there next to her mother, as Margaret crumpled into a heap of despair. Blood thundered in her ears. She hadn't wanted to believe what she was hearing. It couldn't be. Praise God, not her da.

He had been invincible. But his ship was there, anchored in the chilly waters of the bay. And his crew. All the men he trusted with his life. Had he made a fatal error in doing so? And yet, she couldn't fathom how both the crew and ship had survived the journey back home. It was a miracle that no harm or damage had befallen either.

Often, the ships were either burned or confiscated for the plundering party to use in their own fleet.

But there it was. Her da's ship, the *Revenge of Hades*. A little worse for wear, but right in front of her in one piece. Something didn't feel right. Mayhap her da was below deck. He could be hurt and in need of help. The crew had to be wrong.

He couldn't possibly be dead. She had refused to let herself believe that. The Spaniards were cruel and heathen-like. Seonag didn't want to imagine what her da had suffered at their hands.

Today, Seonag still had many questions about what had transpired that fateful day. Had someone in her father's crew betrayed him in the worst possible way? She feared that possibility was true. The question was a crushing weight, lying heavily on her shoulders these past months. The more time that passed, the more convinced she became her da had met his end at the hands of someone he'd trusted that he shouldn't have. Foul play was afoot.

The cool breeze lifted the wisps of her long chestnut hair that had escaped the tight confines of her knit cap, now tickling her cheek. Gray clouds moved quickly through the sky, pushed along by winds coming from the north. A storm was moving in. A ship would be arriving soon, and though she could narrowly make out the form in the distance, she planned to wait and watch it drop anchor.

She prayed it would be the *Revenge of Hades*. Her plan was to follow the bastard captain once he made his way to shore for provisions and ale. After that, she was unsure what her course of action would be.

But she'd made a solemn vow to the memory of her father, and would keep digging until the truth of his death came to light, and justice was meted out to those responsible. Every single last one of them.

She moved a rock with the toe of her boot, shifting it around in the wet sand. Like her father before her, the sea was her home. The thought of living all the days of her life on dry ground held no interest to her.

Her mother didn't agree. Margaret thought she was chasing after a fool's errand.

Maybe she was.

But she had to know the truth—no, she *needed* to know the truth—for her own peace of mind. Unlike her mother, she couldn't let it go and accept the farce of a tale they had been told.

She didn't believe her father's soul could truly rest until justice prevailed.

"Ye know what happened to yer da, Seonag. Let it rest. Please. Let *him* rest." Her mother had pleaded with her when Seonag told her of her intentions to track Jack "Storm" Barr. "I miss yer da with all my heart. Ye're all I've got left. I canna lose ye as well."

The conversation played over and over in Seonag's head. She knew her mother meant well. A pirate's world was no place for a woman, hence her hidden hair and the trews and boots she wore. No more gowns for her. Taller than most women, thanks to her father's massive height, she was still shorter than the average man. But she could easily pass as a teenage boy wanting to join the crew and learn the ways of a crewman.

In fact, her plan depended upon her being accepted into the crew.

She feared it was the only means to uncover what had really happened to her father.

The waves crashed onto the shore, splashing a cool, salty spray on her face, and she watched the white foamy tops breaking apart as they contacted the sandy bottom. Seonag closed her eyes and took in a deep breath, savoring the scent. When she opened her eyes, she spotted the dark form of the ship fast approaching, now almost fully visible on the horizon. The ship was making its way inland. It would be here before long, and if it was the *Revenge of Hades*, its new captain, "Storm," would swagger onto solid ground, head held high. Always demanding the attention that he thought he deserved but had never earned.

She retreated to the line of trees to watch the ship's final approach. If Storm saw her, she wouldn't be able to follow him without notice. She fully expected him to disembark and head straight to the inn. Most of the men did, to have their fill of the things they couldn't get when out at sea.

The laird in charge of this land, a former pirate himself, usually turned a blind eye when pirates docked and came ashore, spending their ill-gotten coin on men's carnal pleasures. Wenches and ale.

Her hands clenched and unclenched into fists at her side as she watched the ship get closer and closer. She narrowed her eyes to view the flag fluttering atop the tall wooden mast.

Dark blue, a skull in the center with a dagger piercing one of the eye sockets.

Her heart sank.

It wasn't Storm or the *Revenge of Hades* as she hoped. This ship was much grander than the one helmed by her father.

But she knew this ship. Knew it well, as had her father.

Seonag sighed. Her shoulders sagged, and despair threatened to overtake her emotions. Still, she watched as the small row boat approached the shore, and waited for the captain to show himself.

Her breath caught.

She was somewhat familiar with the man that commandeered that ship. His reputation preceded him wherever he went.

Someone her father had known well. Someone of whom he'd always spoken highly.

Tall and lean with a strong jaw and chiseled chest, the mere sight of him had her weak in the knees. He was golden and beautiful, not usually the words she would use to describe a man, but she couldn't think of any others that captured his essence. He moved closer to shore, yelling orders to his remaining men, and the baritone rumble of his voice ignited a fire deep in her belly.

His sun-lightened hair long enough to touch his broad,

tanned shoulders, and when he stepped out of the boat and planted his boots into the wet sand, Seonag couldn't take her eyes away from him.

Honey Harris truly lived up to his reputation.

CHAPTER 2

*C*olin "Honey" Harris looked out over the dark blue water of Lunan Bay as Peggy, his quartermaster, guided the *Hella* to shore. The wooden rail he leaned on as he scanned the sea was warm under his calloused palms.

Countless weeks had passed since he'd stood on solid ground, and he yearned to feel the sand beneath his feet, even if it was only for a short while.

He couldn't believe how long it had been since he'd seen his old friend, Lochlan "Chaos" MacLean. Too long. He'd missed him. Missed their easy banter. Their kinship. And their loyalty.

The former pirate and member of the Amadán, was now landlocked at Redstone Castle in Lunan. Lochlan had turned over the Galleon ship the *Hella* to Colin when pirating was no longer his first love. Colin couldn't understand how Lochlan could stay away from the sea. Lady Isobel was indeed one hell of a lass, since she managed to keep Lochlan away from the thing that, at one time, he'd loved more than life itself.

No lass would ever keep Colin away from the sea, of that,

he was sure. He'd swear on his very life that no woman would ever have such an impact on his life.

On land or not, he couldn't wait to see his friend, and since they needed to restock and let off some pent-up energy, now was as good a time as any.

"Cap'n," Peggy called from his position at the wheel. "We'll be dropping anchor soon."

"Good," he said. "Have a few men remain on board to help finish securing things. I will take my leave with the others when we've finished and we'll make our way to the inn. In the meantime, the rest of ye can go have yer fun in town."

"Aye, Cap'n. That we will. Dinna fash yerself about it." The man laughed, his broad smile showing a missing side tooth that only added to his character. He'd lost it in a brawl on one of their stops ashore.

"Not too much fun." Colin harrumphed. "I dinna need to be paying the townsfolk for belongings of theirs ye've all damaged."

"One time." Peggy cackled with laughter, holding his index finger up in the air. "That happened one time, and ye havena let us live it down since."

"Just remember my words." Colin pierced him with a stern look. "I mean it."

"Aye, Cap'n." He locked the wheel in place before calling over his shoulder, "drop anchor!"

"Anchors away!" A crewman answered back, and Colin heard the creak and clank of the chains as the heavy weight dropped into the water with a splash.

There was no port in Lunan Bay, so they had to anchor in deep water and then take turns catching a ride to land on a small rowboat. By the time all the men had disembarked, Colin and the rest of the crew had finished their duties. They dropped into the boat, eagerly anticipating what—no, who—was waiting for them at the inn.

Once they reached land, he swung his long legs over the side and stomped onto the shore, ignoring the bits of water that seeped through, wetting his feet. He should look into purchasing a new pair of boots while he was here if time permitted.

The sparse rays of the sun seemed to seek him out, blinding him, and he held up a hand to shield his eyes as he surveyed the path in front of him.

As he trudged through the sand, he saw a young lad dart behind a tree. Colin couldn't help but chuckle. His reputation preceded him. Young lads always seemed to come out of the woodwork whenever he was in port to try and convince him that they were good enough to be a member of his crew. To be a pirate. He was admired by many. And the knowledge of that, for someone like him, was truly humbling.

And just as every other time, a group of boys trailed along behind him as he walked toward the inn. Wasn't there an old children's tale that followed the same theme? He couldn't remember.

The young lad who hid behind the tree fell in line behind them, being careful to remain near the back of the pack.

Once inside the inn, Colin watched as he faded into a corner. He was an odd one, preferring to be alone instead of part of a group. The rest of the lads paid him no attention.

Music filled the room, and from the laughter and singing, everyone seemed happy and well entertained. There wasn't a man without a drink in his hand and a wench on his lap.

Well, except the young lad whose eyes appeared to be glued to Colin, though he sat in the corner, trying to act nonchalant.

Maybe he was intimidated by Colin's crew.

He wouldn't be the first. Probably wouldn't be the last, either. His men were loud and boisterous, but he couldn't fault them.

Not tonight.

They all deserved a chance to blow off some steam after a tough time on the water. But, he would have to make sure they didn't get too out of control.

Sweeney, one of his crewmen, held a captive audience of men and women from town. He couldn't hear what his deck-hand was saying, but his story was animated, his hands moving non-stop. Suddenly, he hopped up on the table, sloshing ale over the rim of his mug.

Sweeney swept his arm above the crowd, his voice raising. "And dinna ye fash yerselves, Cap'n Storm, who's only captain because of his treachery, will soon meet the wrath of our beloved Cap'n Honey!" He stomped his boot on the table. "To Honey," he shouted, lifting his mug in a toast.

What the hell? His men knew to keep tight-lipped about whatever plans they may have ahead.

How dare he speak out of turn. Colin seethed, his blood boiling. "Sweeney!" He boomed. "Get down at once. Ye've had enough."

The man paled at the fiery anger Colin blasted him with. "Cap'n." He scurried off the table and lowered his voice. "I meant no harm."

Colin pierced him with a steely gaze. "Ye canna be shouting our plans to the world. Ye took an oath. And have broken it. Take yer arse back to the *Hella*. I dinna want to see ye for the rest of the night."

"But, I havena spent any time with the lassies," Sweeney whined.

Colin shrugged. "Ye should've thought of that before ye started telling our secrets. Ye dinna know who here may be loyal to Captain Storm. Now, go before I make ye regret ever stepping onto my ship."

"Aye, Cap'n." Without another word to anyone, Sweeney

came down from the table, stalked to the door, and slipped outside.

Colin emptied his cup of whisky in one long swallow and slammed the cup on the table, scanning the room as the liquid burned through his chest. All eyes were on him.

"Weel, what are ye waiting for?" Colin yelled, holding his cup up for a refill. *"Slainte mhath!"*

A cheer rose, and his men went back to drinking and wenching. Colin could only hope everyone was too far in their cups, or were not interested in Sweeney's performance, to understand what his little speech had alluded to. He didn't need any trouble. At least not now.

Exhausted from lingering in the shadows and discouraged from learning nothing new, Seonag headed for the door. She was just stepping out into the night when one of the men stood on a table and shouted a name. A name that always tasted bitter on her tongue whenever it crossed her lips.

Captain Jack "Storm" Barr. The monster she was convinced was responsible for her father's death. And the *Hella* and Honey were going after him.

Talk about being in the right place at the right time. How had she gotten so lucky?

Almost immediately, an idea sprang into her head—she needed to find a way to join their crew.

Her plan was far from foolproof. She was confident she could pull off posing as a boy.

But she was not sure she could manage the manual labor needed for life on board a ship. She would have to. She didn't have a choice.

Honey would think she was a wee runt due to her size, so she would have to convince him that she was fit for the job.

She could only hope that if he allowed her to be a part of his crew, and that was a big if, that he assigned her to clean or work in the galley.

It took a lot of nerve to walk up to the captain, especially with a serving wench hanging all over him. She had wanted to wait until he finished with the barmaid instead of interrupting him, but it looked as if he could sit there with the woman who so aptly held his attention with her well-endowed assets, all evening or move to an upstairs room for the night and then she'd never get a chance to talk to him.

Seonag's mission couldn't wait.

She couldn't wait.

What she wanted to ask was too important.

She watched his blue eyes darken to a stormy gray as he gazed at the woman with pure lust. Seonag's belly fluttered. Oh, how she wished a man would look at her in the same manner. A wish that wouldn't happen anytime soon, seeing how she was dressed as a boy.

She cursed her errant thoughts and concentrated on maintaining her ruse.

CHAPTER 3

There was no shortfall of wenches to warm Colin's bed for the night. The one draped all over him like a cape got up when another wench with large breasts overflowing the top of her dress shot her a stern look as she sidled over to him, pitcher in hand, and refilled his cup.

She flashed him a smile, and sat on his lap. He smiled back.

She wasn't a stranger.

"It's been a long time since ye've been here, Honey." She stuck out her bottom lip in a full pout.

He nipped the air. He wanted to draw that pouty lip into his mouth and suckle it.

"I've missed ye." She thrust her chest into his. "Did ye miss me? Or just these?" she asked, rubbing her ample breasts against him.

"Aye, Morag." He dipped his head and kissed the swells of soft, milky white skin she offered. Wrapping his arms around her waist, he pulled her closer to him. "I've been gone far too long."

"Shall we take this elsewhere?" Morag cooed.

His scalp tingled as she threaded her fingers through his hair. He vaguely registered someone nearby clearing their throat as he continued to nuzzle the breasts offered to him.

"Ahem."

A tap on his shoulder had him lifting his head and scowling at the lad standing next to him.

"Excuse me, sir?"

Colin let out an exasperated breath. "What do ye want?"

"Ye're Captain Harris, right?" It was the lad he'd observed earlier. The boy was so young that his voice had yet to change.

"In the flesh," he said, then drew his tongue up the bountiful cleavage resting right in his face.

The boy shifted from one foot to another, his eyes darting back and forth between Colin and the wench sitting on his lap. Morag's soft bottom was grinding on his swelling cock, making it difficult to ignore her. He was ready to drag her upstairs and satisfy his lusts.

"Well, what is it ye want?" he ground out, his patience wearing thin. He and Morag had business to attend to.

"I'd like to join yer crew," the lad said quietly, and Colin looked him up and down and then barked out a laugh.

The lad was mayhap ten and four if Colin was being generous and skinnier than the rails on his ship. "I'm in no need of additional help."

"Please, sir. I can—" He paused, bit his lower lip in the most unmanly way, and looked as if he was trying to come up with a reason why Colin should give him a spot on his crew. "I can cook."

"We've got a cook. No need for more than one."

"I, I, I can clean yer ship for ye." He nodded matter-of-factly. "I can mend. Surely, ye have garments that need attention."

Colin was losing patience. Never mind the fact that all the

tasks he'd offered so far were not things one expected to hear from a lad. He had a willing woman sitting on his lap, ready to spend the night lost in carnal desires. And the boy, who was in dire need of a meal by the looks of him, would not leave them alone.

"I want to be a pirate," the boy blurted. Then he looked down at his small boots, before making eye contact with Colin again. His blue eyes were wide.

Colin had a feeling the lad was gifted with the trait of persistence, and wasn't going to leave him alone anytime soon. So, with a sigh, he kissed each breast being offered to him before lifting Morag off his lap and sending her on her way with a pat on her round bottom. He tilted his head and watched her walk, smiling as her arse swayed back and forth provocatively, teasing him as she widened the space between them.

"Sit down," he commanded, with more bite than intended. Too bad. His cock was hard, and he was uncomfortable, and the only thing to ease his pain was now on the other side of the room, pouring ale into another man's mug.

The boy started and stumbled into the empty wooden chair across from him. "Yes, sir."

"What's yer name?"

"Seo—Sean, sir."

Colin narrowed his eyes. "I had a friend named Sean." The lad's quick intake of breath had him questioning what the boy's true intent was. "Yer age?"

"Twe—Ten and six, sir."

Colin gazed at the lad. "Dinna lie to me, and stop calling me 'sir.'"

"Ten and five, si—sorry," Sean answered as a blush tinged his pale cheeks pink.

The lad was daft. No doubt he was being untruthful.

15

Colin would wager his next booty on that fact. No chance he was ten and five. Ten and two? Mayhap.

"Yer parents?"

"Dead."

Colin grunted. An orphan. With nowhere to go and no parents to support him, the boy didn't have a true future. Colin could understand the need to find a replacement for the family he missed.

"Daybreak on the morrow," Colin heard himself saying. "Meet me on the beach. Don't be late."

"Yes, sir!" Sean bounced up. "Sorry." He cringed, then scurried around the table and out the door.

Colin sighed. He was certain he would regret this decision later, but he had a soft spot for children, and one seemingly as lost as Sean was his biggest weakness. Only time would tell how well he would fare on the ship and with the crew.

The crew. He sighed again. They'd not be happy, taking the boy on. Nor about having to teach him the way around the ship.

He had no idea what job he could task Sean with. The lad was way too small for anything labor-intensive. Mayhap having him help out in the galley wasn't such a bad idea. Duncan might argue otherwise. If the boy could truly cook, which Colin had no way of knowing at this time, it would be a nice improvement from the marginally edible fare Duncan made.

The limited meals weren't entirely Duncan's fault. They were vastly underwhelming because of the small number of rations they could take on their voyages. And variety wasn't something they had the luxury of when they were out on the open water.

At least in the galley, the boy wouldn't hurt himself or,

worse yet, get himself flung overboard, which, gauging from his size, was a good possibility.

Colin drained his cup and looked around. The wenches were all busy with his men. Mac, one of his crew, caught his attention and raised his glass in salute before taking a sip and nuzzling the slender neck of the redhead currently straddling his lap.

He smiled back and stood, stretching his legs, and headed out into the night air. He had a room, but wasn't ready to retire. As he sat on a bench placed near the door, he wondered where Sean went for the night. The lad more than likely bedded down in the nearby woods. A danger in itself, as Colin was confident the boy wouldn't be able to defend himself if bandits happened to come upon him.

Not that the lad would lose much. He didn't look to have much worth stealing, but sometimes it wasn't about what the thieves could take, but about what harm they could cause.

Colin wanted to curse again when he caught himself worrying overmuch about the lad and his situation. "Damn it," he cursed under his breath. "Pull yerself together."

Mayhap he should go back inside and help the wenches serve the townsfolk. Suddenly, he seemed to be lacking all his masculinity.

He stood and walked along the narrow pathways. The town of Lunan was quite small, and they were under the protection of Laird Lochlan MacLean. "Laird" sounded funny to his ears. He never expected Chaos, the pirate name he'd been known as, to settle down with a wife and lands of his own, including a castle.

Colin had hoped to see Lochlan while they were here, but he only had this night to restock their provisions before setting sail in the morning. Since he hadn't seen his old friend yet, he suspected his message hadn't arrived in enough time to arrange for a meeting.

"Ye look as if someone just stole yer puppy," a firm voice boomed from behind him.

He recognized the voice right away and turned with a smile. "I was thinking ye were too busy to pay me a visit."

They approached each other and shook hands, clapping each other on the back. "And miss seeing my favorite pain in the arse? Nay. I got caught up working on some repairs, and couldna get away until now." Lochlan laid a hand on his friend's shoulder. "Let's have a drink."

Colin nodded, but instead of heading back to the inn, his good friend led him toward the castle set high on the bluffs, overlooking the North Sea. In the Great Hall, Lochlan swiped a pitcher full of ale from a nearby table and two mugs before dropping into one of the massive chairs near the fireplace. He pointed for Colin to join him.

"How's the *Hella* treating ye?" Lochlan asked.

He had worked on Lochlan's crew for a few years, when his friend was granted the land promised to him from a mission gone awry. Colin would always remember the day Lochlan had asked him to take over the helm of the *Hella*. Despite his doubts about being the right person to master the ship and its crew, his former captain was confident in his abilities and would not take no for an answer. Colin would be forever grateful for the education he'd received under Lochlan's command.

"She's a fine vessel," Colin said with a smile. "I thank ye for trusting me with her." He worked hard to do the job right, to make his friend proud, and never to give Lochlan reason to regret entrusting him with the *Hella*.

"I canna think of anyone more fitting," Lochlan said. "I've no doubt I made the right choice."

"Ye dinna know how much that means to me," Colin admitted, then took a long swallow of ale. "'Tis a dream I never thought would come to be."

"Jesus, what are ye yammering on about? We're talking like a bard."

Colin threw his head back and laughed. It had been way too long since he'd had reason to do so.

Glancing around the Great Hall, he took in the colorful tapestries hanging in front of the long, narrow windows. The pine rushes scattered on the stone floor, and the walls tinged red due to the castle's sandstone, hence its name. The tables were scrubbed clean. A lady was definitely running the keep.

"How's Isobel?"

Lochlan's face softened at the mention of his wife's name. "She's well. She's visiting her ma."

"I'm surprised ye dinna have any wee bairns running afoot."

"'Tis not for lack of trying." He waggled his eyebrows. "I ken they'll be along soon."

Colin chuckled. "I've no doubt."

"How about ye? Ye usually have a line of lassies following ye around, hanging on yer every word. Dinna tell me ye're losing yer touch. Ye'll need to change yer name." Lochlan chortled at his own joke.

Colin shrugged, ignoring his friend's jab. The ladies seemed to have taken well to his new position. Well, if he were honest, he'd had no issues with them prior to him becoming captain. No complaints from him in regard to that. Except for tonight. But that was the lad's fault. Not his own.

"My plans got—" he paused and finished his ale. "Interrupted."

"Ye dinna say?"

"Aye, by a young lad looking for work on the *Hella* approached right as I was about to... Well, let's say I was interrupted and leave it at that."

Lochlan raised a brow in question. "I know naught of any lads looking fer work."

"He was quite insistent. Didna ken the meaning of no."

"Did ye offer him something?" Lochlan tilted his mug back for a long swallow.

"Aye. I've no idea what yet, but I told him to meet me at first light on the morrow."

Lochlan shook his head. "Still have that soft spot. No wonder they still call ye Honey. 'Tis no' just because of the lassies."

He took the pitcher and refilled both their mugs. "Ye and I both know that's no' the reason for the name."

"Well, ye surely didna live up to it tonight." Lochlan slapped his knee, laughing so hard tears sprang in his eyes.

His friend sure was proud of himself. Honey looked at him with a frown and clutched his heart, feigning an attack on his ego.

"Ye continue to laugh. Shall we talk about how yer nickname came about, *Chaos*?" He asked, referring to the moniker Lochlan received after a botched mission.

Lochlan stopped laughing and leveled him with a stare. "Let's just drink to future fortunes."

He held up his glass in salute, and Honey did the same. The origin of their nicknames no longer a topic of interest.

CHAPTER 4

*I*t was still dark the next morning when Seonag woke to meet Honey and his crew at the ship. She had slept little the night before. There were too many thoughts running wild and rampant in her head. They didn't cease long enough to allow her to relax and sleep well.

"Do ye know what ye are doing, Seonag?"

"Aye, Ma."

Margaret worried her lower lip with her teeth. It was on the verge of bleeding, judging by the redness of it. "I dinna like this. 'Tis improper."

Seonag rolled her eyes. "I'll be dressed as a boy." She finished plaiting her hair, made easier now since she'd had her mother shear off a good length of it—something else that made her mother unhappy—then coiled it and tucked it under her rough woolen cap. "See?"

"'Tis exactly what I worry about." Margaret observed her daughter's appearance and shook her head. "If that captain ye're after believes ye're a lad, then he's got a head full of rocks."

"He may think me a wee runt of a lad. I'll make it work. He's going after Storm."

"Why?"

Seonag shrugged. "I dinna know. I missed that part of the conversation."

"I fear if ye do this, child, I'll ne'er see ye again."

Her mother was going to drive her mad. She understood Margaret's concern, but she needed to do this. "I need to find out the truth about Da. This is the only way. I promise I'll be fine." She packed a few belongings into a small satchel, turned to her mother, and stopped short. "Ma, dinna cry."

Margaret sniffled, wiping her nose with a worn handkerchief. "I canna help it. My heart aches at the thought of losing ye."

Seonag dropped her satchel on the bed and embraced her mother in a strong hug. "I'll send word when I can." But even as the words left her mouth, she wasn't sure if they were true. "I promise to be safe."

With one last peck on her mother's cheek, Seonag snagged her belongings and walked out the door into the cool morning air, refusing to look back for fear of changing her mind.

She hated breaking her mother's heart, but she needed to find the truth. No matter what it was. She would do her darnedest to be safe because she had no intention of dying. That was one promise she could keep.

The first light of dawn peaked over the water, making it look like a large inky mass, when Seonag made her way to the sandy beach. Honey's men took in her appearance with partially concealed laughter.

"What are ye doin', lad? Ye lost?" one man asked as he

hefted a sack over his shoulder and limped toward the ship. Seonag noticed the smooth piece of wood replacing the lower half of his right leg. Straps tied tightly above his knee held it in place. She had never seen anything like it.

"Get out of here," another man ordered, swiping his red hair out of his eyes. "We have work to do."

"Cap'n Harris told me to meet him here at first light." She tried to deepen her voice, but it sounded odd even to her ears.

"Fer what?"

She crossed her arms and planted her feet in the soft sand. "He's going to give me a job on his ship."

There was a moment of silence before the men threw their heads back and roared with laughter. "Doin' what?" one asked when he'd caught his breath. "Sweeping?"

"I dinna think ye're funny. I'm stronger than I look."

"Really?" Both men asked in unison.

She nodded at the one with the long, shaggy hair.

"Then step up and make yerself useful. Ye can help us load up."

Seonag approached the pile of supplies the men were loading onto the small boat. It would take several trips to get everything on board the ship. Most of the crates were too bulky for her even to attempt to lift, so she didn't bother.

Hopefully the sacks, though large in size, weren't too heavy. She grabbed the corner of one and pulled. It didn't budge. She tugged with as much force as she could muster, and the bag hardly moved. She tried rolling it toward her. That didn't work either. Defeat wasn't an option, and she kept trying. She needed to prove that she would be an asset to the crew and not a hindrance.

The man with the wooden leg limped toward her. "Mayhap ye should try loading the cannonballs." He dipped his head in the direction of a medium-sized stack of black iron spheres. Her eyes widened. The crew would load the cannons with iron balls and use them to attack other ships. The amount of damage they could do had to be immense.

Fear began to settle in the pit of her stomach. This was all too real. Not some story her father had told her as she listened in awe. Was she really going to do this? Would she be able to pull it off?

She needed to stop questioning herself. And remember why she was doing this.

Steeling herself, she bent to pick up a cannonball. Looks were deceiving. For something of its smaller size, it really shouldn't be so heavy. Or slick. The surface was rutted, but it slipped out of her grasp as she tried to lift it.

She backed away moments before the cannonball landed on her foot. Surely, it would have crushed it and rendered her immobile.

Behind her, she heard the men laughing, talking amongst themselves about how she was going to prove to be useless on the ship.

"What was Honey thinking?"

"Och, ye know he's got a soft spot for those in need. Look at the lad. He's underfed. Honey wouldna have turned him away."

"Aye, but he's another mouth to feed. He's too weak to be of any real help."

Seonag blew out an exasperated breath and tried to block out the conversation happening around her. She struggled to move the cannon balls and was making no progress but refused to give up. She had to prove herself worthy.

"Sean," a familiar voice called, but it took a few long moments before she realized he was talking to her.

She straightened and turned. His massive height had her putting her head all the way back so she could look up at him. "Aye, sir." She bit her tongue, having forgotten once again to not to address him by the moniker he disliked. When she'd spoken with him yesterday, she hadn't realized he was so tall. Broad? Yes. His shoulders were massive. But his height hadn't caught her attention since he'd been seated the whole time they'd spoken.

And she was taller than most women, but he made her feel tiny. Between him and his men, how was she ever going to survive being part of the crew?

CHAPTER 5

*C*olin watched the lad as he struggled with various tasks relating to loading the ship and eventually failed with each one. It was obvious that physical labor was not the boy's strong suit.

"Come with me, lad."

The boy's eyes widened.

"Ye're fine. Leave the supplies to the men."

"But I can help."

Colin chuckled. "I think it best we leave the hauling to the crew. Let's get ye on the ship."

They walked side by side to the edge of the water. The lad was just a wisp. He had to take two steps to equal Colin's one. Duncan wouldn't be happy, but he could think of no other place besides the galley where the lad would be of use.

He entered the water to walk the last few paces to the boat and was ready to climb in when he noticed Sean wasn't with him. "Well, what are ye waiting for? Ye scared to get yer toes wet?"

The lad jumped into action and hurried after him. "Sorry, sir."

"I told ye, dinna call me 'sir.'"

"Sorry." They got into the boat, and Mac grabbed the oars and began paddling them to the *Hella*. At the ship's side, Colin pulled himself aboard with little effort and then turned to Sean, offering a hand. The lad placed his small hand in Colin's, and Colin shook it off, grabbed his arm, and hefted his slight weight on board with no effort.

"Thank ye," Sean said quietly.

"Follow me. I'll give ye a quick tour."

The boy followed close on his heels as he made his way below deck.

Colin guided him to a small room. "This is our storage room. It's where we keep our food and ale. The door is usually locked, and Duncan and I are the only ones with a key."

"Who's Duncan?"

"One of my best men, but he also serves as our cook. At one point, I had the men taking turns, but we soon discovered none of them could cook anything worth eating besides Duncan, so now he's the cook, whether he likes it or not." The *Hella's* previous cook had decided to stay in Lunan with Lochlan. Colin hadn't the slightest idea what he was doing now.

"I can cook, hopefully as well as he can."

"So ye've said. I'll put yer skills to the test. Lord knows, the meals Duncan feeds us are nearly inedible." He continued walking. "The galley is over here."

Duncan was hunched over the table, knife in hand, when they walked in. He paused mid-slice and narrowed his eyes at Sean. "Cap'n. Who do ye have there?" He pointed the knife in Sean's direction.

"I've brought ye some help."

"I dinna need any help."

The man was right. Duncan had been a member of

Colin's crew since the beginning of him taking ownership of the *Hella* and he was more than capable of feeding the crew with no help. Working alone hadn't hindered Duncan in the past, but that didn't mean an additional hand wouldn't be beneficial.

Colin leveled him with a stare. "Ye do need help. He says he can cook. Mayhap, ye can learn from each other."

"But…"

Colin turned and planted his palms on the table, looking Duncan square in the eye. "But what? What is it ye have to say?" Colin was in no mood to deal with insubordination. "Ye know where the shore is if ye canna follow orders."

"Aye, Cap'n."

Colin nodded. "That's better. He'll start tomorrow. I'm going to show him around the ship today."

He led Sean out of the galley and down the hall to the men's quarters. Hammocks hung from rafters, and pallets were strewn everywhere. "This is where ye'll sleep," he told Sean, then continued down the narrow hallway until they came to his captain's quarters. He opened the door and walked in, then waited for Sean to enter.

The lad assessed the room, taking everything in, eyes wide. The large four-poster bed, the writing desk in the corner, the navigational maps on the walls. He walked up to those, showing an interest in the coastal routes.

"Ye can read?"

His head bobbed up and down. "Aye. And I know numbers as well."

"Do ye now?"

"I do. My da made sure to educate me in those areas. He said all good men needed to know those things."

"Yer da was a smart man."

"He was," Sean agreed with a sniffle.

The last thing Colin wanted was to have the lad start

crying, so he quickly changed the subject. "How well can ye read?"

Sean wiped his nose with the back of his hand. "Verra well."

"Read to me."

"Excuse me?"

He dipped his head in the direction of the shelf that held a pile of various documents and missives. "Grab something and read it to me."

The boy bit his lower lip—such an odd trait for a lad, Colin thought—as he shuffled meekly to the stack of papers and picked up the one on top. He perused it over and then glanced at Colin over the top edge of the paper and cleared his throat.

"The eighth of March, the year of our Lord one thousand four hundred and eighty-five. Dear sir—" he paused and eyed Colin apologetically. "I'm only reading what is written."

Honey was impressed as he listened to the boy read the missive he'd received.

"The ship ye previously inquired about, *Revenge of Hades*, has been located near Aberdeen," Sean continued.

"That's enough. Ye're right. Ye read verra well. Especially for a lad so young." Colin observed the boy shift from one foot to the other anxiously. Something didn't seem quite right with the boy, he seemed overly nervous as if he were hiding something, but he didn't pose a threat to anyone, so Colin chose to ignore the nagging feeling he had. At least for now.

"Ye'll stay in here with me."

Sean's eyes widened. Was that fear? "But...the men's quarters?"

"They arenae going anywhere. Yer reading skills will be of use to me. I'm in need of someone to audit my books. When ye're done with Duncan in the galley on the morrow, come back here, and I'll get ye started."

Mouth agape, Sean said nothing before snapping his mouth shut and nodding.

Colin's books were in pristine condition. He kept meticulous notes and needed no help with his logs. But keeping Sean within arm's reach allowed Colin to keep an eye on the lad and get to the bottom of why he really wanted on his ship.

He learned early on in life to trust no one at first glance.

CHAPTER 6

Seonag breathed a sigh of relief when Honey left her to oversee his crew. She'd nearly cried out when he stated she would be staying in his quarters with him. Pray tell, what was she going to do? If she slept with the rest of the men, she assumed she'd be able to blend in. They'd all be too busy to pay her any attention.

But with her and Honey locked in a room together? She couldn't think of a worse scenario. Why, oh why did she have to tell him she could read? And do numbers? She was in this awful situation because she couldn't keep her mouth shut.

"Och!" she sputtered in the empty room and then remembered the letter she was reading before Honey stopped her. She walked over to the desk where the letter sat and picked it up. It had mentioned her father's ship. Sitting in the chair, she read on.

As you suspected, the ship is being manned by Storm Barr, Sean's former quartermaster. The Revenge of Hades *doesn't appear to have suffered any damage and looks clean on all sides. My contact said he heard talk of a stash of gold coins hidden some-*

where on the ship but did not see it with his own eyes. The ship continues to head up the east coast of the North Sea.

"Bastard," Seonag swore under her breath. The letter did not refer to why Honey wanted the information, yet she knew he had a reason. His man had alluded to it last night before Honey quickly gave him the boot.

She wondered what the reason was. But in the end, it made no difference to her what his reasoning was. He was tracking down the man that she would see dead.

Not for one minute did she believe her father's death was caused by the Spanish.

Especially since the letter mentioned gold coins. Seonag knew her father had been transporting a great treasure when his ship was attacked, but hadn't known what. If it were the Spanish, they would have taken possession of the gold, not leave it to the crew of the captain they'd slaughtered. Past actions dictated they wouldn't necessarily kill the entire crew, but would enslave a few of the stronger crewmen and use them for hard labor until they died of exhaustion. Either way, no one would have made it back to Lunan Bay.

Storm had to have been after the gold on the ship. Even though her father was a pirate, Sean was an honest man. He had been hired to transport the treasure and get it to its final destination, wherever that was supposed to be.

But Storm was a selfish knave. This letter confirmed her thoughts on the matter.

Storm killed her father to gain possession of both the *Revenge of Hades* and the gold.

She would offer Storm the same fate he had offered her father.

Death.

~

That evening, Honey brought in a pallet and blanket for Seonag to sleep on. She watched him with wide eyes as he set the pallet on the floor near the far wall on the opposite side of his massive bed. If there were something that would give up her ruse, it would be this situation.

"There's an empty shelf in the cupboard next to ye. Ye can use that to store yer belongings. They'll be safe there. The only person allowed in here besides me is Peggy, and now ye, but he never goes past my desk." He reached his arms back and grasped his shirt before pulling it over his head.

Her breath caught. This was improper. But she couldn't avert her eyes. His smooth skin was tanned a lovely golden color from many days spent in the sun. It looked as if it would be warm under her palms if she touched it.

This was wrong. She should look away.

But she couldn't.

He sat on the edge of the bed and took off his boots, placing them neatly beside a small table tucked against the wall. Then he stood, and in one swift motion as her heart pounded in her chest, he whisked his trews off and Seonag audibly gasped. She quickly covered her mouth with her hands and scrambled under the blanket and faced the wall, but not before she'd gotten a full view of Honey's perfectly muscled buttocks.

Even with her eyes closed, she could still see them. They were seared into her memory. What a beautiful man he was. Oh, how her mother would not approve of the compromising position in which she'd suddenly found herself.

"Ye all right?" Honey asked from his position on the bed. *His naked position.*

"I'm fine," she squeaked. Not turning around to face him. If she did, she feared he'd see her face aflame from embarrassment. She'd never seen a naked man before, and his image, in all its glory, was scorched into her brain.

In the future, she would need to ensure that she didn't react. Would a boy react? She didn't think so. They saw each other naked all the time, didn't they? It would be the same as if she'd seen another woman's body.

After a bit of time passed and no more words were spoken, Seonag heard Honey blow out the candle, and they were suddenly enveloped in darkness.

In her youth, when she'd dreamed of her future, she'd never envisioned her first night spent with a man would entail her sleeping on the floor dressed as a boy. Though one could argue that she wasn't truly spending the night with a man if they weren't in the same bed together.

She didn't care. This was the closest she'd ever been to a man that wasn't her father. She lay there, lulled into a sense of relaxation from the ship's gentle rocking as it maneuvered deftly over the waves. With each passing nautical mile, she was getting closer and closer to the man that had killed her father.

How she would get Storm to confess to what he did, she was unsure, but she would. Her father would have justice.

The ship was surprisingly quiet, considering the amount of men onboard. Even the water splashing along the sides was only slightly audible. She listened to Honey's breaths as they became slower and were soon replaced with the softest snore she'd ever heard. Her father could rattle the rafters with his snorts and whistles as he slept. It was funny the things she remembered about him that made her smile.

Sleep didn't come for her that night. Her mind raced with scenarios yet to come and how she could continue to play this part without her true identity being discovered.

If tonight was a preview of what was yet to come, she would surely need to rein in her reactions to Honey.

She knew that was what was needed. But would she be

able to keep her composure when he was so close she only had to reach out her hand to touch him?

CHAPTER 7

*C*olin woke at the break of dawn, then sat up, stretched, and glanced over at Sean. The lad looked as if he still slept. He faced the wall, wearing the same clothes and hat as the day before. The boy was a bit odd but pleasant enough.

After dressing, Colin splashed his face with cool water from the basin and patted it dry with a square of linen.

"Sean," he called.

The lad sat straight up, dragging the blankets with him, covering his chest even though he was fully dressed. Colin shook his head in surprise at the boy's unconventional reaction.

"'Tis time for ye to rise. Get ready and meet Duncan in the galley. He'll need yer help this morning."

Sean nodded in agreement. "Yes, si..." he paused, biting his lower lip. "If ye dinna want me to call ye sir, what should I call ye?"

"'Captain' works just fine," Colin tossed over his shoulder as he walked out the door. "I want ye in the galley in five minutes."

"Yes, Captain," the faint voice answered as he headed to greet his crew for the morn.

"Mornin' Cap'n," Sweeney called out. "Where's the lad? Did ye throw him overboard for his uselessness?" He chortled, slapping his knee.

Colin was on him in an instant, grasping his tattered linen shirt. He pinned him against the wall, lifting him off his feet. "Ye're wearing on my verra last nerve, Sweeney. Ye'd best not forget who it was that took ye in as an abandoned, scrawny lad and gave ye a chance," he ground out between clenched teeth.

The deckhand's eyes widened in fear and he nodded, his head banging the wood panels with every move. "I meant no harm, Cap'n."

Colin dropped him to the floor and looked at his crew that had begun to gather around. "We all have our own stories of how we came to be where we are now. No' one of us has had an easy path. Remember that. The only thing we can do is lend a hand when someone needs it. The lad has no one. We're his family now. If any one of ye have a problem with it, I'll put out the plank."

"Aye, Cap'n," Sweeney muttered before slinking away.

Colin didn't have the patience to deal with petty complaints or insubordination. If a member of his crew didn't want to follow his rules, they were no longer needed. He ran a tight ship. His men worked well together. If one person thought they were going to insert themselves and start trouble, they'd find themselves treading water and hoping they came across another ship before the sea creatures found them.

"Back to work," Colin barked at the men lingering about. They scattered. No one wanted to be in the path of his wrath. His nickname might be spot on with the fairer sex, but when it came to his men, "honey" was the last word he'd use to describe himself.

Peggy was at the helm when Colin climbed to the quarterdeck. "Trouble this morn, Cap'n?" He asked.

Colin scanned the horizon. The water was calm, the sky a dull blue but clear. "No' anymore," he answered with a smirk.

Peggy shook his head and smiled. "Sweeney, I'm guessin'?"

"Aye, it seems always to be Sweeney."

"Ye need to give him a break, Honey. His mouth is bigger than his brain."

"True, but he needs to know when to reel it in. Some things are best thought and no' spoken."

"He'll learn soon enough."

"He's had long enough. He was part of Chaos's crew before mine. He's no' new to this life. He knows the rules. If he canna follow them, he can get off my ship. And I willna think twice about it."

Peggy nodded. "He'd be stupid to cross ye."

"Any news on the *Revenge of Hades*?"

"No. The last sighting we had put them in Aberdeen and still heading north, so that's where we're going. We'll catch up to them."

Colin grunted. "I'm going to kill that bastard once I get my hands on him."

"And I'll be right there with ye."

He looked out at the water. A pod of dolphins broke the sea's surface and swam alongside the *Hella*. They bobbed in and out of the water as if leading them to their final destination.

Sean Ruane, the former captain of the *Revenge of Hades* hadn't deserved to die at the hands of his most trusted crew member. Sean was a good man with a family that loved him. Colin couldn't imagine what they were going through without Sean to take care of them. He'd wondered about them many times even though he'd never met them. Sean spoke about them often whenever he and Colin met up.

The story Storm had spread about Sean and the *Revenge of Hades* being attacked by the Spanish was utter rubbish. Anyone with sense could see right through it. If the Spanish were going to attack for the gold, they'd have taken the gold, killed the crew, and burned the ship. They wouldn't kill the captain and then leave the crew and ship to go on their merry way.

He was surprised that Storm was daft enough to think anyone worth their weight in salt would believe his farce of a story.

And from what Colin had heard, the gold was still somewhere on the ship. If he could prove that, he could prove that Storm was a killer and avenge his long-time friend. Whether he threw Storm out to sea or ran him through first, he still had to decide. It was something he pondered many a night as he lay in bed.

What he knew for certain was that in the end, Storm would be dead. Colin looked forward to being the one to bring him down to his knees. There was nothing worse than being betrayed by one of the people you trusted the most. If you couldn't trust your crew, you couldn't trust anyone.

Storm was lower than the scum that grew on the surface of stagnant water. It remained to be seen if the rest of Sean's crew was in on the coup or if they were serving under Storm for fear of repercussions. He would find out if any of them had played a hand in Sean's death—if so, they would meet the same demise as Storm.

CHAPTER 8

*S*eonag waited until she was sure Honey wasn't going to return to the cabin before jumping up and refreshing herself. She was becoming increasingly uncomfortable from having her breasts bound and wished she could loosen the binding for a bit, but there was no time. She let down her hair from her cap and run her fingers through it, clearing away any tangles. Her scalp loved the freedom, and she massaged it a bit before begrudgingly replaiting her hair into a coil and stuffing it back under the cap. She headed out the door.

When she walked into the galley, Duncan looked at her as if he didn't know who she was. She ignored him and leaned against the table where he worked, and observed what he was making. "Ye're baking Pandemayne?" she asked, referring to the dough he was kneading. Seonag was impressed. That particular type of bread was usually only made for the wealthy.

"Aye, are ye familiar with it?" he asked, flipping the dough, then pushing his palm into it and rolling it forward.

"I am." She pushed up her sleeves, grabbed one of the balls, and began kneading alongside him.

They soon fell into a natural rhythm and before long had all the Pandemayne kneaded and set aside to rise.

"Do ye ken how to use a knife without slicing off one of yer fingers?" Duncan questioned.

She rolled her eyes and snatched a knife from the table. "Of course I do."

"Good. The apples need peeling and slicing."

Looking around, she spotted a crate filled with apples. "Where did ye get these?" She knew apples were out of season.

"One of the ships we raided not too long ago had a cache of them," he answered as if that was perfectly normal.

She guessed it was in their world. She shouldn't be surprised. How many times had her father come home, bringing her an item from a faraway land that wasn't something they could have sourced locally?

They worked mostly in silence for the next two hours, preparing the food for the crew to break their fast and readying the food they would cook for the evening meal. Duncan kept to himself unless he was barking out an order, but she believed he was enjoying the help.

"Ballocks," Duncan hissed as he grabbed his hand.

Seonag glanced over and immediately sprang into action at seeing the bloody trails streaming between his fingers. She grabbed a stack of linens and rushed over.

"Let me see."

"'Tis fine," he murmured as he squeezed his hand.

"'Tis verra well no' *fine*," she parroted and grasped his hand. "Let go so I can take a look," she demanded.

He did, and she nearly fainted. The cut was deep. Deep enough that she could see the white bone in his finger. She swallowed the lump in her throat and wrapped a strip of cloth tightly around his wound. "Do ye have needle and thread?"

"Do I look like a seamstress to ye?"

"Hold this and dinna stop applying pressure. I'll be right back." She ran out of the room in search of what she needed. The supply room was locked, so she continued on. She needed to find Honey. She turned the corner and ran right smack into Sweeney.

"Watch yerself, ye little runt," he spat.

She ignored his insult. "Do ye know where Captain Honey is?"

"Mayhap. Why do ye want to know?"

"I dinna have time to play yer games." She stepped to the side to go around him but he grabbed her roughly by the shoulder and stopped her from moving forward.

"What do ye need him for?"

"I dinna have to answer to ye." She tugged her shoulder free and resumed looking for Honey. She found him as he was descending the stairs from the quarterdeck. "Captain."

His brows furrowed as he took in her flustered state. "What's wrong?"

"I need, um, I need a needle, thread, and whisky if ye have any."

"I have all that, but what happened?" He spun her around when she started back toward the galley. "Lad, take a deep breath. Talk to me."

"It's Duncan. He's cut himself in the worst way. I need to sew his hand up to tamp the flow of blood."

"Follow me." They hurried to his quarters and collected a spool of thread and a needle. "Take these to Duncan. I'll grab whisky and catch up with ye."

She nodded, and as she walked away she remembered something else and stopped. "I'll need a flame, too."

Honey dipped his head in acknowledgement and said, "I'll be right there."

In the galley, Duncan was sitting on the floor, slumped against the wall. She ran over and knelt beside him. "I'm back." Loud footsteps behind her let her know that Honey was there, too.

"Here's the whisky."

She took the flask from him and handed it to Duncan. "Take a long swallow. Ye're going to need it."

While he did as he was told, Seonag placed his hand in her lap and gently unwrapped the blood-soaked cloth. She looked at Honey. "Can you heat the needle over the flame until it's verra hot?"

He nodded. She retrieved the flask of whisky from Duncan and poured a splash over the wound.

"Argh!" he ground out from the pain.

"I'm verra sorry."

"Here's the needle." Honey carefully handed her the long piece of steel.

"Thank ye," she said, then poured a wee bit of whisky over the needle to ensure it was clean, and then gave the flask back to Duncan. "Drink the rest of this."

Then she went to work. Gently as she could, with the needle threaded, she brought the skin together and started stitching with one hand. With every piercing of his skin, Duncan bit out a curse. She flinched with each one, but couldn't blame him. Her stitches were crude, but they would suffice to staunch the bleeding.

"Can ye pass me a square of linen?" she asked Honey. "Tear another one into strips, please."

She wrapped Duncan's finger tightly and tied it in place with the pieces Honey passed to her. "Ye should rest up."

Duncan struggled to his feet. "I'm fine. I've got food to prepare."

"Ye're a wee bit pale, Duncan," Honey admitted. "It may be best for ye to take some time to gather yer wits."

"The men need to eat," he quietly said as he slumped against the wall for balance.

"I'll see to the preparations and getting the men fed. No one will miss their meal."

Both men narrowed their eyes at her, their mouths set into thin lines.

"The lad's right, Duncan. Go rest."

"Cap'n, I—."

"Now!" Honey boomed. "That's an order. Sean will finish the meal."

CHAPTER 9

*C*olin helped Duncan regain his balance and walked with him back to the sleeping quarters. If he didn't lead him there himself, he had no doubt that Duncan would find something else to do.

While on the way, Colin couldn't help but think about how Sean had taken charge of the situation. He'd handled it with the ease and the poise of someone much older. And Sean's skill with a needle and thread left Colin with more questions than answers. He was impressed.

After handing Duncan the refilled flask of whisky and watching as he climbed into one of the cots swinging from the rafters, Honey left him to check in with Sean.

He found the lad still in the galley, looking over a large pot of something boiling on the fire.

"Where did ye learn how to mend wounds like that?"

Sean jumped and squealed in surprise.

"I'm sorry. I didna mean to frighten ye."

With a hand over his heart, the boy nodded. "I didna hear ye come back in. How's Duncan?" His breath came in shallow bursts.

"He'll be fine." Colin took note of the blood smeared on the front of the lad's clothes. He crossed his arms, knitted his brows, and watched the lad work. "I'm still waiting for an answer."

Sean looked at him questioningly. "Excuse me?"

"How did ye learn to mend wounds like that?" It wasn't a task that men, let alone young lads, usually performed. Odd for a lad of his age.

"Oh, um, my mother taught me."

The way the lad wouldn't meet his eyes and the redness of his cheeks were giveaways that he was lying.

"Yer mother was a healer?"

"What? Oh, um, no. She enjoyed sewing her needlepoint. I would sit and watch her."

Ballocks. He didn't believe Sean's explanation. No lad was going to sit and watch his mother sew when he could be outside with his father learning the tasks of men.

Sean struggled to move the pot from the flame. Colin stepped over and helped him. He had no strength. He was positive the boy was being untruthful. He just did not ken his reason why.

"The men can come in and get the food to break their fast. Let's go clean up."

The lad's eyes opened round and wide, the blue darkening, but he didn't say anything, only nodded his head and followed Colin out the door.

Back in his quarters, he opened the door to his cupboard and reached for a clean tunic. He turned to Sean. "Do ye have another shirt?"

Sean nodded and went over to his assigned shelf and selected a shirt, but made no move to change. Colin pulled the dirty tunic over his head, unfolded the clean one, and brought it down over his shoulders, tugging at the hem to straighten it out.

"What's the matter?"

"N-nothing." Sean paused, biting his lower lip. "Would ye mind leaving so that I can change?"

Colin was taken aback. "Are ye daft? Change, so we can get back to work." He turned to his desk and started to go through some of his papers, but the boy didn't budge.

"Could ye please go?" he asked quietly, eyes lowered to the floor.

He didn't have time for games. Colin turned to chastise the lad, and his words caught in his throat. Sean was pale. Understanding hit him as if a punch to the gut.

Of course. That would explain why Sean was always so weary around his men.

He hadn't asked how long ago that Sean's parents had passed. But it seemed by the size of him that he'd been living without a home and regular meals to eat for quite some time.

No doubt he'd come across some unsavory characters as he wandered the streets.

Had the poor lad... Colin couldn't even finish the thought in his head.

Big, blue eyes pled for him to leave the room.

Colin might be well known for his ruthless attitude among his fellow pirates, but not when it came to those wronged and less fortunate. His heart broke into pieces whenever someone had been mistreated. Especially a child.

Another reason why he was recruited into the Amadán— the secret band of mercenaries fighting for good and meting out justice in the name of those harmed. Lochlan was one of his Amadán brothers.

Colin hissed. At the same time, his blood heated at the thought of the bastard who had hurt the lad.

"Who was it?" he asked quietly, his voice barely above a whisper as he tried to keep his raging temper from boiling over and scaring the lad even more than he already was.

Sean looked at him, shadows darkening his petite features. "I, uh." He clamped his mouth shut, shifting his weight from one booted foot to the other. "I dinna understand yer question, sir."

He let the "sir" slip. The lad was already traumatized enough. "The person that caused ye harm. Who was it?" he ground out the last question. His fury rising, causing his nostrils to flare.

Sean's eyes widened even more before he once again focused his gaze on the floor. "'Twas nobody. I simply prefer my privacy, if ye don't mind," he said quietly.

The ship suddenly listed to the right and they both scrambled to steady themselves. Sean's small hand grasped the bedpost to stop himself from tumbling to the floor. Colin listened for his men's call, but didn't hear anything. He knew he should check to see what was happening, but he wanted to continue this conversation.

Torn between his duty to his men and the lad that had been through so much, Colin swore under his breath and turned toward the door. He paused, resting his hand on the knob, and said quietly, "I do hope one day ye will trust me enough to tell me yer story. Until then, please know that no harm will come to ye while ye're under my watch."

Sean said nothing, and Colin forced himself to open the door and walk out, allowing the boy to change his clothes alone as he'd originally wished.

≈

Finally on her own, Seonag blew out a long, exasperated breath. If Honey had stayed in his quarters any longer, she'd have given up her farce. She quickly undressed and dipped a clean corner of her shirt into the water in the basin and wiped down her arms, and washed the remnants of dried blood away.

She'd washed her hands earlier after Duncan and Honey had left the room, but with so much to do to get a meal ready for the men, she hadn't even thought to check the rest of herself for evidence of the stitches she'd sewn.

She folded her soiled shirt and set it aside. Did pirates launder their dirty items? Judging from what she'd seen so far, they didn't. She'd change that at once. They were surrounded by water, for God's sake. Would it hurt them to haul up a bucket or two and clean their clothing?

Not in the least. Her mind made up, she contemplated unwrapping the binding flattening her breasts because it was becoming increasingly uncomfortable, but knowing that Honey could return to his quarters at any moment and see her made the decision not to do so easy.

But she did tug on each side of the linen strips, trying to loosen them up a wee bit. At least that would lessen some of the constriction while still not showing her breasts.

Hastily, she slipped a clean shirt over her head and glanced at herself in the looking glass hanging on the wall. A stray lock of hair peeked through, so she tossed her cap on the bed and quickly redid the plait before putting her hat back on and tucking any stray wisps under the rim.

With a last look, she drew in a deep breath and walked out of the chamber, determined to find Honey and insist that he have the men bring water on board for cleaning.

As Seonag made her way to the main deck, she passed Sweeney, and he halted her advance by grasping her arm, spinning her around to face him.

"What are ye up to, boy?" He bent low, so they were eye to eye. His wretched breath overwhelmed her senses, making her want to vomit.

She tried to pull her arm away, but his fingers dug into

her flesh, making her want to cry out, but aware she couldn't without giving away that she was a woman.

"I know ye've got a dastardly plan whirling around in that little head of yers. We've no use for ye here."

"Sweeney!" boomed a familiar voice from the end of the hall.

The crewman paled and let go of her arm immediately.

"Dinna ye have a deck to swab?" Honey asked.

"Aye, Cap'n. I was on my way to do that."

"Then I suggest ye stop harassing the new help and tend to yer own duties."

"Aye, sir." As he passed to make his way to the deck, Sweeney gave Honey as wide of a berth as the narrow hallway allowed.

"Sweeney," Honey called after him.

The man paused and turned to look at Honey but remained silent.

"Keep yer hands to yerself. If I see you manhandling the lad again, ye'll be swimming with the fishes."

"Aye, Cap'n," Sweeney said while scrambling up the stairs and disappearing above deck.

"Are ye unharmed, lad?" Honey's voice was filled with concern, his forehead creasing as he looked her over.

Seonag nodded, but didn't dare speak. She didn't trust herself to say anything. She was relieved Honey had appeared when he did.

"Where are ye off to?" Honey asked.

"To the galley, Cap'n," she answered, finding her voice. The area they called a galley hardly passed as one, but it was an area that allowed them to prepare food, so a galley it was.

He nodded, studying her face.

She felt as if he could see into her very soul. And if he could see the thoughts running around her head, he'd kick her off the ship.

"I have to get back to the men. Let me know if ye need anything, lad."

And with that, Honey turned on his heel, and she was alone once again in the hallway. She would have to be warier of Sweeney. He seemed to be the most unsavory character she'd ever had the displeasure of meeting, which surprised her because Honey looked to be the type of man that would only hire honorable men to work on his crew. Mayhap he saw something in the weasel that she didn't.

She walked to the galley, swaying slightly with the boat. The gentle rocking calming her nerves after the off-putting encounter with Sweeney.

He was an unlikeable man, and so far she'd found each of their meetings unsettling so.

He was someone she would need to keep her eye on.

That afternoon in the galley, Seonag was taking stock of the items they had on hand when Mac entered and studied her silently while he leaned against the wall.

"Can I help ye with something?" she asked, placing the trenchers into a low cupboard and straightening.

"Nay, just seeing how ye're faring, lad." He chewed on a piece of straw tucked into the corner of his mouth.

"'Tis been an exciting day, to say the least."

"Aye." Mac agreed. "I'll leave ye to yer duties. I know ye've work to do."

As he turned, Seonag noticed the tear in his tunic.

"Mac?"

He turned. "Aye?"

She dipped her head in his direction. "If ye bring yer tunic to me later, I can mend that tear for ye."

He raised a brow in question and looked over his shoulder at the tear. "Ye mend, too?"

Seonag shrugged.

"Ye are an odd lad, Sean," Mac said. "I'll drop my tunic off to ye this evening."

Mac left, and she was once again alone.

Had she made a mistake, admitting she could sew? She sighed aloud in the empty room. Since they were on a ship, her cooking skills were limited. The lack of variety meant there wasn't much for her to prepare and cook. Mending would keep her mind occupied.

With nothing left to do in the galley for the rest of the day, she decided to check on Duncan. She hoped he wasn't angry with her for commandeering his duties. The last thing she wanted to do was take his work away from him.

But Honey had commanded he rest to regain his wits. That wasn't something she had suggested.

Before Seonag made it to the sleeping quarters, she spotted Duncan in deep conversation with another crewman she didn't know the name of. It was no surprise to anyone that he wasn't resting.

She cleared her throat, alerting the two that she was there.

Duncan eyed her and furrowed his brow. "I knew ye couldna handle feeding the men. What do ye need help with?" He asked, a triumphant smile lifting the corner of his mouth.

"I've no need of help," she answered, and the smile on the man's face turned into a frown. His reaction was unnerving. "All the men are fed for now, and I've tidied up the space. I was ensuring ye are feeling well."

"Och, aye, I feel fine, lad." He held up his hand, the dressing showing a bit of blood seeping through. "'Tis naught but a small cut."

"I thought ye'd be resting as the captain instructed."

Duncan roared with laughter. "Because of this? Nay. I've had much worse."

She nodded. "Weel, I was only checking. I'm glad ye've almost recovered." Seonag left the men to get back to whatever conversation they'd been so engrossed in when she'd interrupted them.

She needed to find something to do. She felt restless. Every crewman had an assigned job, but she had nothing.

Mayhap she would go back to Honey's cabin and tidy things up a bit there. He wouldn't mind that she didn't think.

Standing in the doorway to Honey's room, her hands on her hips, Seonag surveyed the area. The stack of papers she'd read from the other day beckoned her to study them more closely. She was tempted.

She knew there was the letter regarding Storm, and it piqued her interest, but she also felt as if she were prying by reading further without Honey's permission. Mayhap she could find something else of interest to read in the pile of papers on his desk? Something that didn't allude to whatever his future plans were. A weather report. Anything to stifle her boredom.

As she thumbed through the stack, the letter about Storm beckoned her, but Seonag didn't stop. She'd found out all the information she needed reading the parts aloud to Honey when he'd asked.

"What am I doing?" Seonag whispered to the empty room. Feeling ashamed, she stepped away from the desk, leaving the papers as she'd found them, and examined the space that fit Honey perfectly.

Her pallet looked out of place when compared to the

solid wood furnishings filling the area. The huge bed took up most of the space, and it was piled high with throws. Seonag's skin heated at the memory of seeing Honey's bare buttocks as he undressed.

"Sean?"

Seonag jumped at Mac's booming voice filling the room, a high-pitched squeal escaping her lips. Hands on her chest, she tried to slow her breathing as Mac looked at her, eyes narrowed in an unspoken question.

"Mac. I didna hear ye approach."

"Ye seemed to be lost in thought, and didna hear my knock."

Seonag nodded. "I apologize. Do ye need something?" she asked.

With a sheepish grin, he held out not one but several tunics. "I know ye offered to mend one, but do ye think ye can stitch these up as well?"

She took the pile from him and studied the items. Most were basic tears. Repairs that wouldn't take much skill, but would keep her busy until it was time to return to the galley.

"Of course. I'll have these fixed for ye soon."

"Thank ye, lad."

After Mac left her alone to get started on the sewing, Seonag went on the hunt for needle and thread. There were none in the desk drawers. A chest that almost reached the ceiling in height beckoned her from the far corner. She tested the knob, and to her surprise, it turned, and the door swung open.

She paused, her senses assaulted by the masculine scent that was all Honey. The chest smelled like the forest and the briny salt of the sea. A beautiful blend of two usually separate areas, combining Honey's two worlds.

Inhaling deeply, Seonag scanned the items in the chest, trying to ignore Honey's personal items that she didn't have any right to be rifling through. In the far corner, a small wooden box caught her attention.

She glanced over her shoulder to the door. There was no sign of Honey or any of his crewmen in the hallway outside the quarters. Though her intentions were innocent, a sense of guilt filled her, and her heart beat faster.

Her mother had always told her she was much too curious. To a fault.

Fighting the pull to open the box and study the contents inside, she scanned the rest of the shelves but didn't find any thread.

Closing the doors, she blew out a breath. Where else would Honey keep needle and thread? She could go to the galley and use the needle and thread she'd sewed Duncan's finger with earlier, but there wasn't much thread left. Though the needle was bulkier than what she needed, it would still serve the purpose.

She made her way to the upper deck, thankful she didn't cross paths with Sweeney. Unease swept over her every time she was in the man's presence.

Snagging the needle, now clean of blood from Duncan's wound, Seonag also grabbed what little was left of the thread.

"Where are ye off to?" Honey's deep voice startled her as she descended the steps to go below deck.

Lord! How all of these rowdy men could be so quiet when approaching her, she had no idea, but they'd managed to sneak up and scare her several times today.

The man was unbelievably quiet for his size. She paused and turned. He stood at the top of the stairs.

"Um, I was, well, since I canna offer much help in the running of the ship..." Seonag felt her cheeks heating under his intense gaze. "I thought I might help by mending some of the men's clothes. I've got Mac's to do now, but I'm sure others could use some stitches."

Honey shook his head, a small smile brightening his tanned face. "Ye have an odd set of skills for a lad, Sean. I'm sure the men will be thankful not to have holey clothing."

"Do ye have any more thread? I only have this wee bit that's left over from earlier." She held up the thread in the palm of her hand to show him how much she had available.

"Aye, follow me." Honey descended the stairs and walked towards his quarters, the scent of the sea rolling off his skin and infiltrating her senses. She couldn't help herself; she closed her eyes and breathed in with a sigh.

"Ye coming?"

"Oh, yes, sorry." Seonag needed to clear her head before he thought her even more peculiar.

Back in their quarters, Honey approached the shelves on the far side of the room. Reaching to the highest shelf, which Seonag noted was way beyond her reach, he grabbed a small satchel and handed it to her.

Opening it, Seonag found a needle perfect for mending and enough thread to get her through plenty of projects.

"Thank ye. I'll get right to work on these." She pointed to the pile of linens needing mending.

He nodded, but his gaze lingered, and she began to shift from one foot to another. She felt exposed. That was how intense his gaze was. Her cheeks heated, and she silently cursed her body for its betrayal.

"Cap'n!" someone called from somewhere outside the room.

His face lightened, and it seemed to snap him out of his thoughts. Who knew what he'd been thinking.

"Do ye require anything else?" he asked but didn't stay to hear her answer.

She watched him leave, his long strides taking him

quickly out of the room and back to his crew. Her whole body was warm. For someone who had such a fearful reputation, she'd only seen the softer side of him. Honey was truly a fitting nickname for him. Yes, she knew the moniker referred to his reputation with women, but he'd been nothing but sweet and kind with her since she'd imposed herself on his ship.

Sitting in the large chair, she threaded the needle and got busy with the task she knew she was more than capable of doing.

For the second time in as many days, the needlepoint her mother had insisted she learn proved to be of use. It was mindless work. But it kept her busy and offered her a sense of being without getting in the way.

Before long, Mac's shirts were mended. She smiled and surveyed her work. Her mother would be proud.

The shirts needed a good cleaning too, but without the requisite supplies she couldn't wash them so she folded them neatly and went in search of Mac.

She still had to talk to Honey about what items he could bring on board to keep the ship and the men as clean as possible. But she also knew bringing up the conversation would only add to the already odd opinion he had of her.

By now, he surely thought something was wrong with her. Her attempt to pull off being a young lad wasn't going as planned. Seonag had wanted to fit in more, but as the time passed, she knew her chance of success was very low.

One thing she was certain of, though.

She would make Storm pay for her father's death.

CHAPTER 10

$\mathscr{C}$olin leaned over the railing and watched the sun
glint off the water, sparkling like a gem in its dark
depths. What a beautiful sight to see. Bringing the spyglass to
his eye, he scanned the distance, looking for the ship he was
chasing. They were sailing farther north, and according to
Colin's sources that was the final destination of the *Revenge
of Hades*. But he couldn't see her yet.

They were traveling at a good clip, and it wouldn't be
long before they'd close in on their target. He looked forward
to the encounter.

He would show his friend's family that Sean wasn't
forgotten.

Family.

The word felt bitter on Colin's tongue. At times he longed
for a family of his own, and yet, he knew the sea and the life
he lived had no place for one.

He protected families. He made sure they were well taken
care of when they were torn apart.

It was his sworn duty as a member of the Amadán.

Yet, the thought of his own family was always in the back of his mind.

But he couldn't think about that now. He had work to do. That was why he was on this mission. Not only to make the bastard pay for killing his friend, but also for the family that Sean had left behind. He didn't ken how they were living now. Hell, he didn't even know their names. Sean had talked about his family often, but was very careful about giving out too much information about his wife and daughter. There was always a danger in doing so and one could never be too cautious.

He could imagine how they must be struggling without Sean there to provide for them.

It couldn't be easy for a widowed woman and her daughter to find enough coin to survive. Unless they came from wealth—but Colin had never got that impression in all the talks he'd had with Sean.

The coin that Sean had been transporting on the *Revenge of Hades* would more than pay for the family's living expenses and set them up with a nice life. Colin just had to get to Storm before he spent the booty or stashed it away.

"Any sight of the *Hades*?" Peggy asked, leaning against the rail.

Colin shook his head. "Nay." He looked through the spyglass again, scanning the horizon, seeing nothing but never-ending sea. "We must be getting close."

"Aye, she's a slower ship. It canna be long now."

Off in the distance, a swell of water lifted and a huge beast broke through the surface, causing large ripples that rocked the ship. The creature blew out a huge burst of air from the top of its head, spraying water in a large radius around him.

Colin waited, watching, and was soon rewarded with another beast surfacing, performing the same action.

"'Tis a beautiful sight," Peggy commented.

"Looks like a family. Let's hope they stay clear of the *Hella* while we pass." They surfaced again farther away, and Colin blew a sigh of relief. He didn't want anything causing a delay in their chase and continued observing the beasts as they swam away from the ship, breaking the surface in even intervals.

The wind picked up, blowing Colin's hair into his face. Gray puffy clouds filled the sky. "A storm is approaching. Let us use the wind to our advantage."

"Aye, Cap'n." Peggy hobbled away, barking out orders as he went.

Colin was thankful for Peggy's loyalty, but the man was more than capable of leading a ship and its crew. It was just a matter of time before he commandeered his own.

Colin peered through the spyglass one last time, wishing the *Revenge of Hades* would appear in the distance. But luck wasn't on his side, and all he could see was the ocean, far and wide. Folding the contraption, he tucked it into his pocket.

"Holler if ye see anything. I'm going to check on Sean. It seems our new recruit is quite the seamstress."

Peggy raised a brow in question but said nothing as he manned the helm, steering the ship in the direction that hopefully would take them to Storm and, along with him, the *Revenge of Hades*.

Colin observed his crew as he walked the length of the ship on his way below deck. Each man was performing his assigned duty. He was fortunate in the crew he'd chosen. Each man served a crucial part of the team, and they all shared a common goal...freedom and riches. But they each served with a code of honor.

Those of lesser means were not easy prey, as some pirates he knew saw them. No, Colin didn't want to take from the poor. He had his eyes set on big purses.

And it was even better when those purses came from men who had received said gold from ill-conceived tactics.

Descending the stairs, he saw Sean round the corner. "Sean," he called out, and the boy froze in place. Colin sighed. He'd shown the boy nothing but kindness. He wished Sean would stop shrinking in fear whenever Colin approached him. "Where are ye off to, lad?"

Sean turned, folded tunics in his small arms, which reminded Colin that he really needed to work on putting muscle on the lad. He would be of no use to the crew if they couldn't build up his strength.

"Cap'n." The boy bent in what looked like a half-curtsy, before catching himself and bowing his head.

Such an odd person Sean was.

He held up the tunics in his arms. "I was just on my way to bring these to Mac. I've finished mending them."

Colin narrowed his eyes at Sean. "Show me yer work." He didn't really have any interest in the stitching, but for some reason that he couldn't explain, Colin didn't want the lad to leave his presence just yet.

That feeling was unnatural. He was not a bugger of lads. So, what was it about Sean that appealed to him? Was it Colin's need to protect him? The boy was surely in need of protection. Of that, Colin was in no doubt.

But it didn't explain the pull Colin felt toward him. It made him question his sanity. Sean shuffled from one foot to the other but nodded. He grabbed the first tunic on the top of the pile and tucked the rest under his arm, then unfolded the material and pointed to the spot he'd mended and silently passed it to Colin.

Colin accepted the offered tunic and inspected the job Sean had done. The stitches were small and neat. He couldn't recall a time he'd seen a man do so well at such a feminine task.

He nodded and handed the tunic back to Sean. "'Tis mended verra weel. Yer mother taught ye that, eh?"

"Y-y-yes, Cap'n," Sean stuttered. "Before she, before she passed." He sniffed.

Och, he didn't need him to get sappy. 'Twas bad enough the lad didn't seem to have a manly bone in his body. Colin smiled. "I'm sure Mac will be verra happy with yer skill indeed. Carry on."

Sean nodded and stepped away, but then turned back to Colin, worrying his lower lip—which Colin noted was becoming pink and puffy.

"What is it?"

Sean inhaled a deep breath as if he were preparing himself for a huge undertaking. "Mac's tunics are dirty."

"Aye, an unfortunate consequence of the sea."

"I thought I might take over laundering the men's clothes." Sean looked up at him with round, blue eyes, the color swirling like the clouds on a stormy day.

Colin didn't want to look away. And it took all of his might to drag his gaze away from the depths of Sean's eyes. Jesus, he needed a drink.

"What did ye have in mind? Our resources are severely limited, as ye can tell."

Sean bobbed his head up and down. "I understand that, Cap'n. I thought mayhap the men could bring a bucket of water upon the ship, and I can work with that. 'Tis not the same as being on land and freshening their linens, but 'twould be better than the state of their clothing now."

"A bucket of sea water?"

"Aye."

"What will that do? Other than make the men smell like bait for the fishes?"

"If I boil the water, it won't smell as strong as the sea and it will still help to clean the men's clothing."

Colin studied the lad. He was serious. Colin could tell by the stern yet hopeful look on the boy's face.

"Fine. When ye bring Mac his tunics, tell him to fetch a pail of seawater. Do with it what ye will."

Sean smiled, pink tinging his cheeks. "Aye, Cap'n. Thank ye."

"Dinna thank me yet. Ye have no idea how the men will take to ye making them smell like bait."

The boy turned and started walking toward the sleeping quarters.

"Sean," Colin called out.

"Aye, Cap'n?" The boy didn't turn to face him, just stopped his forward advancement.

"After ye bring Mac his tunics, go into my cabin and in my wardrobe. To the left are a couple of items that could use yer skill with a needle and thread."

"Aye, I shall tend to them forthwith."

Colin watched as the lad disappeared around the corner. Conflicting emotions roiled inside his gut, making him question everything about himself. He spun and headed back up the stairs in search of a cask of ale. He needed to drown away the thoughts bouncing around inside his head.

CHAPTER 11

*S*eonag hurried down the hall, quick to get away from Honey's scrutiny. She paused and leaned against the wall, releasing a long breath when she was out of his sight, clutching Mac's tunics tightly to her chest. Her heart beat a steady thrum, and that last encounter with the handsome captain knotted her stomach.

Surely, she wasn't the only one who felt the charge between them? After catching her breath, she hurried to the sleeping quarters and left Mac's tunics in a neat pile on his cot. The room was empty, so she couldn't ask him about the water, but she would inquire the next time she saw him.

Making her way back to Honey's cabin, she did as he'd ordered and opened his wardrobe for the items that needed mending. There were only a few. Her eyes wandered over the contents. Her fingers itched to touch them, even though she knew it wouldn't be right.

But she wanted more insight into the person that Honey was deep down inside. She'd glimpsed the softer side of him. There was more to him than the gruff exterior he put on in front of his crew. He was caring and kind.

Her curiosity almost won, and she nearly rummaged through the articles in the wardrobe, but she managed to control herself, grabbing the items and closing the doors.

She inspected what she needed to mend. A pair of trews, one sock, one tunic. They would be easy enough. Gathering the thread and needle, she sat in the chair at Honey's desk and started on the sock. She turned it inside out and pinched the material together, then added her stitches, making sure they were extra small so as not to irritate his foot. She could only imagine how painful it would be to have a lump in your stocking as you wore your boot. That would cause a sore, and she wanted to prevent that from happening if she could.

After she finished her sewing task, Seonag tucked away the needle and remaining thread in a small box and folded Honey's items, returning them to his wardrobe. Then she headed to the galley to see if anything needed to be done for the men's next meal.

Duncan was sitting on a barrel when Seonag entered. He acknowledged her with a grunt, but didn't question why she was there. She took that as a sign of progress.

Wiping her sweating palms on her trews, she approached and asked what she could help with.

"There's naught for ye to do here, lad," Duncan answered.

"Are ye sure? I've no tasks and want to help where I can."

Duncan tilted his head and studied her a moment.

His scrutiny made her uncomfortable. And nervous. Did he know her secret?

"I heard a rumor today," he stated.

Her heart leapt to her throat. *He knew!* Heat flushed her skin. Would he tell Honey? Surely, he would. If he wanted to keep his captain's trust, that would be his only option.

"What have ye heard?" She asked quietly, scared to hear the words she already knew he was going to say.

"That ye stitch clothes better than ye stitch skin."

She sighed, relaxing her shoulders. He didn't know. "I do have skill with a needle and thread."

"Weel, if that 'tis the case and ye are looking for something to fill yer time, I have some things ye can repair."

"Of course," she nodded. "I'm glad to be of help in any way I can."

"The day is getting late. I'll bring them to ye on the morrow." He stood and filled two cups with ale from a cask in the corner, then handed one to her.

Seonag accepted the proffered cup. "Thank ye," she said before sipping the strong ale. She watched Duncan over the rim of her mug. He had a gruff demeanor, but his brown eyes were kind. He wasn't as muscular as Honey, but he was tall and stocky. He looked to be built like a blockade.

She got the impression that if the ship were attacked, whoever it was that decided to fight Duncan would never make their way past him.

Honey had surrounded himself with a well-equipped crew to support him. A captain couldn't ask for anything more than that. To have a crew that had your back, no matter the situation.

She finished her ale and set the mug on the wood slab that served as the prepping table for the meals. "If ye dinna need anything else, I'm going to retire for the night."

Duncan took a long swallow of ale, emptying his cup, and then refilling. He nodded. "I'll see you in the morn, lad."

Seonag dipped her head in acknowledgment before turning and making her way back to the quarters she shared with Honey. On the way, she passed Mac in the hall.

He greeted her with a mutter that she couldn't quite understand. "Oh, Mac," she called out, remembering she had a task for him.

The man stopped and faced her. "Aye?"

She cleared her throat. She had her order from Honey,

but that didn't mean she felt comfortable giving a command to one of his men. "Captain wanted me to have ye bring a bucket of water on board."

He frowned at her. Probably trying to gauge whether she was serious or not. "Cap'n wants what now?"

"'Tis actually I that wants it, but I did get permission from Captain Honey first."

Mac clucked his tongue, clasped his hands behind him and rocked back and forth on his heels. "Ye need a pail of water?"

"Aye."

"Fer what?"

"Does it matter?"

"It does if ye want me to be yer fetcher. Ye'd do well to strengthen up those sticks ye call arms so ye can fetch yer own damn pail of water."

Seonag looked at her arms and then crossed them in front of her bound chest and stuck her chin out. She was sure she looked like a child but she didn't care. "The water is fer laundering yer filthy linens."

"My linens," he emphasized the word, "are fine. Why are ye so concerned about the state of our clothes anyhow? Dinna ye have better things to fash about?"

Mac probably did find it odd that she was so worried about cleanliness. Would a boy actually care about the things she'd mentioned? Most likely not. She would have to pay more attention in the future. "I'm doing this for all of ye, not myself. Ye'd think ye'd be grateful instead of condescending."

"I'd watch yer tone, boy, if I were ye. Ye may prove to be useful, but no one wants to deal with a sharp tongue."

Seonag caught her breath. She had been a bit forward. *Stupid,* she cursed herself in her head. "Aye. I apologize, Mac. Will ye please bring me a pail of water?"

He harrumphed. "Aye, but only because Cap'n ordered it.

Otherwise, ye can hang off the side of the ship and get yer own damn water."

He barked out a laugh and walked away, leaving Seonag alone to hear his chuckles echo off the walls.

CHAPTER 12

*I*n the next few days, Seonag fell into an easy rhythm. She spent the nights trying not to be distracted by Honey's buttocks when he undressed for bed. Even though he was more careful, they were still sharing a room. There wasn't really any other place for him to undress. And she knew she shouldn't look.

It was sinful, but his body was such a sight to see.

He was beautiful in a manly way that she'd never known. Granted, her experience with men was very limited, yet she was certain that Honey was quite handsome. Margaret had kept her sheltered while Sean was at sea, and when he was home, no men were coming around to pay their regards.

But she couldn't help herself. She watched him through lowered lashes every night as he quickly removed his trews and slipped in between the throws. And she'd only seen him from the backside. She was thankful for that—she wasn't sure she would be able to contain her composure if she got a glimpse of his manhood.

Honey still thought a man had mistreated her in the past, and she'd never corrected him in that thought. She figured that made it easier for him not to be so open with his naked-ness in front of her. Even though she secretly enjoyed it.

Thus, her nights upon the ship hadn't led to much sleep. She was too nervous that her hair would come out from her plait or peek through her cap. She was terrified to unbind her breasts for long moments for fear of being discovered. So ofttimes, her chest was painful. She looked forward to the day that she could be free of the tight wrap.

But that day wouldn't come until she had avenged her father's name. When she looked Storm in the eyes and killed the light in them.

In the mornings, she went into the galley to see if Duncan needed any help. Most days, he said no, and today was no different. She walked in, and he was there hunched over something on the table that looked like dried, crusty bread.

One of the crewmen—Derrick, if she remembered correctly—was sitting on a cask in the corner, juggling four oranges, tossing them in the air in a circle. She'd heard about the jesters in the king's court that held such talent, but she'd never seen anyone perform the trick before.

Seonag stood and watched him for a minute or so before he let them drop and he caught them, two in each hand, and winked at her.

She smiled back. "Where did ye learn to do that?"

He hunched his shoulders. "I taught myself when I was younger. I learned to entertain myself whilst I sat in my room after being punished by my father." His crooked smile was unashamed.

"Ye could work for the king with that talent."

He laughed out loud at that. "The king doesna want me in his court, and just as well, for I would rather die than be teth-ered to the king as his entertainment. He has plenty of bards and jesters for that."

She nodded and dropped her gaze to the floor. "I meant no disrespect," she said quietly.

"Och, Needle," he said, calling her by the nickname the crew had given her due to her sewing skills. "None taken."

"Where did ye get the oranges?" she asked, referring to the fruit he'd been tossing in the air.

"Duncan here was hiding them from us."

"I was doing no such thing. Ye grabbed them off the table when ye came in here to bother me."

"Keep lying to yerself. Ye like the company," Derrick quipped.

"I like being left alone to do my job. Now hand them over." He grunted when Derrick lobbed the fruit over to him.

She looked at the cook. "Oranges are rare. Where did ye get them?" Seonag was especially curious. She hardly ever came across them while shopping in the village. The last place she'd expect to see some was on a ship in the middle of the sea.

"Our last raid. It was part of our booty. We need to use them before they rot."

"Are ye going to make a tart?"

Duncan roared. "A tart? Are ye daft, lad? Our supplies are severely limited. I'll segment them, and each man will get a piece or two."

Her eyes widened. Was she included in that? She'd never eaten an orange before.

"Now, will ye two leave? I've got work to do. Derrick, dinna ye have a deck to swab? And Needle, something surely must be in need of yer stitching."

She and Derrick laughed but left Duncan alone to his duties. As they ascended the stairs to go above deck, Peggy let out a holler.

"Cap'n! Avast ye!"

Honey came thundering down the deck from the oppo-

71

site direction that she and Derrick were coming from. "What is it?" he called.

Seonag noted the thin sheen of sweat on his skin. He must have been working on something before being called up.

"'Tis the *Revenge of Hades*, Cap'n. Up ahead."

With long strides, Honey made his way over to Peggy and pulled the spyglass from his back pocket and extended it, holding it up to his eye and aiming it in the direction his quartermaster was pointing. He dropped it from his eye and smiled at Peggy.

"I knew we would catch the bastard. Keep on her. We should reach her by the morn."

"Aye, Cap'n!" Peggy answered and turned to return to the helm.

Seonag ran to the rail and gazed in the direction Honey and Peggy had. If she squinted, she could just make out a small dark speck, bobbing along the waves in the far distance. No matter how hard she tried, she couldn't tell if it was her father's ship or not. But Honey had confirmed it was, and that was enough for her.

She licked her lips in anticipation.

Soon, Storm would feel her wrath.

Soon.

"What are ye grinning about, lad?" Colin asked as he moved to lean over the railing on his left side.

Sean squeaked, then pressed his lips together. Colin didn't think the lad had heard or seen him approach. That feeling something was off with his new recruit crept up his spine. He just couldn't quite put his finger on it, but it was there, tugging at him.

Before he'd approached and spoken, Sean had looked much wiser than his years allowed. Colin wondered what the boy had been through to cause such an intense look.

"I'm happy ye found yer mark, Cap'n," Sean said, turning to Colin.

He tilted his head as he studied the boy. He seemed unable to contain his excitement. Colin was appreciative of his support, but he seemed a wee bit too enthusiastic about the situation.

"What happens now?" Sean asked, looking at him eagerly, his blue eyes wide in wonder.

Colin looked over the water and took a deep breath, inhaling the salty air into his chest. "Weel, now we close the gap, and when the time is right, we attack."

His mouth opened and formed an O.

"Dinna fash. We will be safe. I promise ye that. Our intent is no' to sink the ship. We want what they are transporting. It doesna belong to them, and they gained it by ill means."

"How so?"

Colin considered how much to tell the lad. They'd become close these past weeks. Sean had read through his missives and had seen his books. He knew Colin's numbers and their supplies. The lad was very bright, even if a bit odd in his talents.

"The former captain of the *Revenge of Hades* was a good friend of mine. He didna deserve the fate he was given."

The lad nodded but remained silent as he gazed at the dark water.

"Are ye going to kill him?" he asked quietly.

"Storm?"

Sean nodded.

"Aye. And every last member of his bastard, traitorous crew."

Sean sucked his bottom lip into his mouth and worried it

with his teeth, a gesture Colin had seen him do often but was so uncharacteristic of a lad.

"He deserves to die."

The statement was a whisper and Colin wasn't sure if he'd actually heard it correctly, but Sean looked at him with such hatred in his eyes, Colin knew he had. He eyed the boy, trying to discern what Sean was thinking.

"Ye know Storm?"

"Nay," he answered quickly. Too quickly.

"Ye seem to have a strong opinion about someone ye've never met." Colin glimpsed Sean out of the corner of his eye, watched as the lad's chest heaved.

"I—if he's done what ye state, then he should pay the price fer that deed."

Colin nodded. "He'll pay with his life. That I swear." He glanced up at the sky. Dusk was fast approaching. "The morrow should be a busy day if we catch up to them as planned."

"Aye." Sean sighed as if he were bearing the weight of the world on his shoulders.

"Dinna think much of it, lad. The *Revenge of Hades* poses no threat to us."

Sean turned away from the water and met Colin's eyes. "I know. I'm going to retire for the night if ye have nothing else fer me to do?"

Colin could probably find some menial tasks for the lad, but he looked as if he wanted to be left alone. "Nay, go to our room. I'll be in later."

Sean dipped his head in acquiescence and pushed off the rail, heading to the stairs that would take him below deck.

Colin watched as he walked away—the lad's gait was somewhat feminine. Colin rolled his eyes and laughed at his daft thoughts. They'd been out to sea too long. And he'd been without a woman for even longer. His mind was running rampant, seeing the fairer sex everywhere he looked.

The lad was a runt. Nothing more. But even as Colin thought that, he also thought with his dainty features, Sean would make a bonnie lass.

"Damn it," Colin muttered to no one in particular. He checked in with Peggy one last time. "How's the track looking?"

"They've sped up their pace a bit, but even so, we're faster. We'll meet up in the morn."

"If anything changes, let me know at once. I'm off to find some whisky."

"That bad?"

Colin laughed. "I canna even voice my thoughts aloud. Ye and the crew will deem me unfit to be captain and take over the *Hella*."

Peggy boomed with laughter. "It canna be as bad as ye think, Cap'n."

"Easy for ye to say that now. Ye've no idea what is going on in my mind." He shook his head. "I dinna believe it myself." He clapped Peggy on the shoulder. "Send for me if needed."

"Aye, Cap'n."

Colin made his way to the galley and the small closet they kept their supplies in. At the door, he fumbled for the key to unlock it. Once opened, he surveyed the items they still had on hand. The shelves were getting bare. It was good that they'd located the *Revenge of Hades*. Many more days on the water, and they'd be scraping for food.

A situation they'd been in before, but it was one he'd rather not have to go through if needn't be.

He grabbed the cask of whisky off the top shelf and tucked it under his arm. After closing it, he relocked the door, then grabbed a cup and took a seat in the corner of the galley. He wasn't ready to go down to his quarters yet.

Sean was there, and he was conflicted. He could sense the lad wasn't telling him everything. Even with their nights spent talking, reading, and going over numbers. Colin had let his guard down around the lad. Something he didn't often do. It showed how much he trusted the lad, but he still that thought that the lad was holding something back from him.

He poured himself a healthy cup of whisky and took a long swallow, savoring the burn as it wound its way down his throat and settled warmly in his chest.

Refilling his cup, he emptied it in another long swallow. As much as he'd like to drain the bottle and get lost in his cups before retiring to his quarters, he needed to keep his mind clear for the fight ahead.

Capping the flask, he stood and set the mug on the table before unlocking the closet, replacing the whisky, and locking the door once again.

The whisky warmed his veins. It thrummed through his body. Nothing disconcerting, more like a warm, enveloping hug from an old friend.

He left the galley and started to make his way to his cabin slowly. He passed Sweeney in the hall.

"Cap'n." Sweeney acknowledged Colin, not stopping and keeping his eyes downcast.

Colin thought that the next time they were on land, he might have to talk to Sweeney and let him go. There was something slimy about the man. He reminded Colin of an eel. Slippery and wily. He did his work, but never all that great, and he didn't take any initiative on his own. He wasn't the type of worker Colin needed on his crew.

And he lacked the morals Colin deemed important in his men.

In his room, the lantern cast a soft glow on Sean's prone

body lying in bed, facing the wall as always. In the nights they'd shared the room, Colin had never seen Sean face the bed where he slept, only the wall.

He stood in the doorway for a long moment, watching Sean.

And questioning his sanity.

CHAPTER 13

Seonag heard Honey open the door. She had lain down only a moment before. She'd taken advantage of the time alone to release her bindings for a bit. Her breasts welcomed the freedom, and she'd almost cried as she bound them again, then slipped her tunic back on and settled into bed.

What was he doing? He hadn't entered the cabin yet.

"Are ye awake?" Honey's smooth burr filled the room.

Seonag had to hide her sigh. His voice sidled down her spine to settle in her belly. The feelings he awakened in her were as none she'd ever felt before. It was good that they'd finally found Storm. If they stayed on this ship together in such proximity for much longer, she feared she might throw caution to the wind and reveal herself to Honey one night on a whim.

"Lad?" Honey asked, his voice a loud whisper.

"Aye," Seonag answered, but she didn't turn around.

Honey didn't say anything, but she heard him enter the room and close the door softly behind him. Listening to the rustle of linens as he drew down the throw on his bed and the slight creak as he sat down. He slid off his boots, a slight thump following each as he set them beside the desk, following the same routine as he had every night before.

She had no experience in undressing a man, but she wanted nothing more than to do exactly that with Honey. To pull his tunic up and over his head, baring his broad chest for her eyes to feast upon. She bit her lip to keep herself from gasping at the devilish thought.

Her mother would most definitely not approve of the thoughts filling her mind. She heard him stand and knew he was removing his trews. Oh, how she wanted to turn around and watch him. He hadn't blown out the lantern, and she was sure his bronze skin would glow golden under the bobbing flame.

She audibly sighed at the image and then clamped her hand over her mouth to silence herself.

"What was that, Sean?"

As if she could tell him what she was thinking—though she really wanted to. She wanted this charade to be over. When Honey found out what she'd done, he would not be happy with her.

One more day.

One more day and Storm would be in her sight, and she could exact her revenge and end his life. She didn't know how, but getting to him was the whole reason why she'd taken on this daft journey. She tried not to think about how little she'd thought the whole thing through.

Storm would overpower her in an instant, she had no doubt. She would have to be smart in her moves. Allow him to get close enough so that she could sink a dagger into his black heart.

But only if she could get within close proximity of him. She wasn't the only one who wanted him to meet his demise.

Honey wanted to see him dead as well.

She knew he was more than capable of cutting Storm down.

And the knowledge that he cared enough about her father to avenge his death warmed her heart even more.

Colin Harris was a good man, no matter the stories she'd heard about how ruthless he was. He'd shown her nothing but kindness since she'd first met him. Well, maybe not the very first time when she took him away from the wench he was more than likely going to bed.

Seonag was surprised at the stab of jealousy she felt at the thought of Honey sleeping with another woman.

She wanted to be that woman. The ship rocked over the waves, lulling her into a sense of serenity. That, and knowing that Honey was in the bed next to her. She felt protected with him there.

Apparently giving up on them having any further conversation, he snuffed the lantern and enveloped them in darkness. She waited for her eyes to adjust, forms slowly taking shape, and listened to Honey's breathing as she did every night when they went to bed.

That night, she did fall into a deep sleep. She dreamed of slipping naked between the sheets of Honey's bed, revealing her true identity to him. In her dream, he wasn't angry with her. He blessed her with a smile so genuine, that it melted her heart. He drew her into his chest, and their skin met, heat exploding between them.

When she woke in the morning, her linens were damp with sweat. She wanted to linger and think about the dreams she'd had all night long. But now wasn't the time.

She turned and glanced at Honey's bed.

It was empty.

For the first time, he had awakened before her and had already dressed and left. She sat up and stretched her arms. Then she hurried to dress.

Today was going to be a great day.

She splashed water on her face and then quickly replaited her hair and tucked it under her cap. Next, she set off to find Honey and see how close they were to the bastard Storm.

As Seonag rushed to the upper deck, she stopped short at the top of the stairs. All the crew was lined up at the ship's rail, staring out over the choppy water. She stood on her tiptoes, trying to see over their shoulders, but she was too short and only saw their backs.

She surveyed the men, found where Peggy was standing, and made her way over to the man.

"What's going on?" she asked as she tapped him on the shoulder.

Peggy turned around. "Ah, Needle. Good morn! At long last, our chase has come to an end. We've caught up to the *Revenge of Hades.*" He stepped aside to allow her to see what all the men were looking at.

Her heart skipped a beat. There before her eyes was her father's pride and joy. The ship that he'd lost his life over. A flood of emotions rushed through her.

Happiness at seeing the ship.

Fury at the situation.

Sadness at the loss of her father.

In her mind's eye, she saw her father when he'd first acquired the ship, making his dream of becoming captain of his own vessel a reality. He was so proud and happy. He'd hugged her mother so fervently that Margaret had squealed in delight.

She turned back to Peggy. "What happens now?"

"Cap'n Honey has put out a call to her captain, requested a meeting."

A meeting. "I thought he wanted the man dead?"

"Aye, he does. But Cap'n is a man of honor. Even to those that aren't deserving of it. He'll invite him to a conversation to discuss the events that led to the coup."

Seonag was confused. Why give him the chance to talk his way out of his past sins? She and Honey both knew he'd done what he did for greed. Storm wanted to be captain of his own crew, and he wanted the booty that her father was transporting.

The easiest way was to turn her father's crew against him and lead a coup. And that was exactly what he'd done. She was sure of it. Her father had trusted his crew with all his being, but apparently, Storm had offered them something they couldn't refuse. Was it the coin her father was transporting? Most likely. Money was always talked about and brought out the greed in men.

Seonag had thought his men were more loyal than that. But she'd been mistaken.

Studying Honey's crew lined up, she realized they all had their hands on the hilts of their swords. It was good to know that Honey didn't overly trust Storm. Trust would get him nowhere with that heathen.

The only thing that bastard cared about was himself.

"Here." Peggy pushed something cold and hard into her hand.

Seonag looked down at the dagger Peggy had given her. The hilt appeared to be silver with vines of ivy carved into the handle.

"I know ye dinna have a sword of yer own. Carry that with ye at all times. Ye never know when it will come in use."

Seonag nodded. "Thank ye." She tested the weight of the dagger in her hand. Shifting it from one hand to the other, the hilt felt cool in her palm. The blade had been buffed to a shine, and the sun glinted off the steel. Looking at it, she could tell it was sharpened to a fine edge.

This blade.

This was what she could use to sink into Storm's heart.

After he'd put out the call for a meeting to Storm's quarter-master, Colin waited calmly along with his crew for Storm to show his pathetic face.

Peggy had done an excellent job tracking the *Revenge of Hades* throughout the night. The maneuvers Storm had used to try to outrun the *Hella* were to no avail, and now they waited to see if he would take Colin up on his offer to meet.

Colin didn't expect the bilge-sucking captain to accept his offer, but following his creed, he had to put it out there.

If Storm refused it, that was on him, but at least Colin would know that he gave the cretin a choice before he allowed his crew to attack and board the ship to take it over.

And take it over, they would.

Colin paced behind his men. His hands were clasped behind his back as he walked back and forth, his sword a friendly companion at his side.

He noted Sean had made his way up to the deck and joined the rest of his crew. The lad had been in such a deep sleep when Colin had woken up that he hadn't had the heart to disturb him. And Colin refused to acknowledge how long he'd sat in his bed and watched the lad doze.

Hours passed, and still Storm didn't show.

Colin was beginning to lose his patience when a whistle sounded, catching his attention. He rushed to the rails and looked over at the other ship. The *Revenge of Hades's* crew was abuzz with activity, which was more than had occurred in the hours since Colin first requested the meeting.

"Cap'n Harris," an unknown voice yelled up to him, bouncing over the water.

Colin planted his boots on the deck and crossed his arms as he waited for the man to continue.

After an unnecessarily long pause, he finally spoke again, "Cap'n Storm will be here momentarily. He apologizes for keeping ye and yer men waiting." The snide smile the man gave him told Colin he was lying, but he let it pass.

He only wanted the bastard to show his face, so Colin could state his intentions.

"I'm waiting," Colin called out, and the man nodded before disappearing below deck. Colin studied the ship. Even though it had been taken over by force, it still looked in good shape. The traitorous crew had been taking care of it. For that, Colin was thankful. He was hoping not to destroy the ship in taking down Storm, but if it came to that, he would. His crew just needed to be able to salvage the precious cargo it carried first.

But it would be nice to be able to add the ship to his own fleet. He could think of one or two men on his crew that would make an excellent captain for her.

At that time, Storm came forward, a sneer crossing his pompous face as he studied Colin.

"Cap'n Harris!" The bastard smirked. "My apologies for keeping ye waiting." He dipped into a low bow, sweeping his black feathered hat off his head in greeting. "I hear ye've been looking for me. I'm honored" He stood straight and splayed out his arms. "Now that ye've found me, pray tell, why the chase?"

"Ye have something that doesna belong to ye," Colin answered.

Storm feigned shock and clucked his tongue. "Such accusations. Ye should watch yer tongue else I make ye eat yer words, Cap'n."

His threat did nothing but convince Colin his gut feeling was correct. "I invited ye to come aboard the *Hella*. Ye have my word that no harm will come to ye during our conversation." How Colin wanted to go against his word and slice him down right there, but he was a man of honor, pirate or not.

A plank was brought out and placed between the two ships. Colin held his breath to see if Storm would cross. The bastard seemed to be contemplating his next steps, but after a long moment, he pushed off the rails and stepped onto the plank. His boots thumped across the wood with every step.

Colin had the urge to pull the plank out from under Storm's filthy, worn boots, but again, hard as it was, he kept his word.

Colin's crew parted and allowed Storm to come aboard. The pirate approached Colin and held out his hand, and as repulsed as Colin was to accept, he did so and gave it a firm shake.

Storm surveyed the deck. "Shall we sit and have a drink? It sounds as though ye've a lot ye'd like to discuss."

Colin didn't trust the bastard as far as he could throw him, so he refused to take him below deck. He snapped at Derrick, and he and another crew member left and then reappeared with a small table and two chairs. They arranged the furniture, then put a flask and two mugs on the tabletop, and backed away.

Colin extended his arm, offering Storm a seat.

Storm narrowed his eyes at Colin for a moment but then sat down.

Colin poured ale into each mug and offered one to Storm.

The bastard eyed the mug warily and then said, "Take a sip first."

Colin sighed and emptied the cup in one large swallow of ale and then refilled it before handing it back to Storm.

"Believe me, if I was going to kill ye, poison wouldna be my weapon of choice."

Storm shrugged. "One can never be too careful nowadays." He looked into the mug and then took a sip before setting it back on the tabletop. "What do ye want, Harris? I know this isna a courtesy call."

"Ye're right about that. What happened to Sean Ruane?"

"Ah, my former captain." He placed his hand over his heart. "May God rest his soul."

Colin slammed his fist on the table. "Tell me what happened."

Storm ran his tongue across his crooked, yellowed teeth in a sneer. "Those bastard Spaniards attacked. Killed our dear beloved captain. It mattered naught what we tried to do. We couldna save him."

"Ye're a lying bastard!" Sean shouted from behind him.

Colin frowned at the lad. What the hell was he doing?

Storm turned to look at the boy and gave him a sinister smile. "Weel, weel, weel. What do we have here? Seonag," he addressed the lad with familiarity. "What the hell are ye doing dressing like a lad?"

What?

What the hell was Storm talking about?

Storm shifted his gaze back to Colin. "Judging by the surprise on yer face, Harris, I believe ye didna ken ye had a lass on board." He pushed his chair away from the table, the legs scraping loudly against the floor of the deck. "I'll be getting back to my ship now. Ye let me know if ye have any more questions."

"Ye killed him."

Storm spat at the boy, "Ye dinna know what ye are talking about, ye stupid lass. And I suggest ye hold yer tongue before I remove it from that pretty little mouth of yers."

Before Colin could comprehend what was happening, Sean launched himself at Storm, but Peggy caught him and pulled him away. He fought against Peggy, his arms and legs flailing to escape the strong grasp.

What the hell had just happened?

Colin was so confused at this turn of events, he let Storm climb back onto the plank and reboard the *Revenge of Hades*.

And then, the realization hit him like a ton of stone. The effeminate way Sean moved. His small bone structure.

He wasn't a runt.

He was a goddamned lass.

Colin had never felt so betrayed in his life.

Sean—no, what had Storm called her?—Seonag looked at Colin, pleading with her blue eyes. For what? Understanding. He shook his head. *No.* He turned away from her.

"Honey," she cried. "I can explain."

He held his hand up to her to stop any explanation. "Dinna. I dinna want to hear a word from ye."

His heart beat so strong that he could feel the pump in his chest. He felt...humiliated.

"Mac." he shouted.

"Aye, Cap'n."

"Lock her up below deck. I dinna want to see her face right now."

"Honey, no." Seonag cried. "Please, no. We both want the same things."

He glared out at the water. At the ship opposite them. At the bastard Storm as he stood there, cross-armed, laughing at him.

"Get her out of my sight!" he ground out.

"Right away, Cap'n." Mac answered and grasped Seonag by the arm and pulled her toward the steps that would lead them below deck.

"No." she yelled, trying to slap his hands away, but she was no match for the burly man.

He picked her up, threw her easily over his shoulder in the position she hated most, and hauled her down the stairs as if she were no more than a sack of flour.

CHAPTER 14

*I*n the past couple of weeks that Seonag had spent on the ship—exploring, cooking, helping those who needed it—she had never come across the room she now found herself locked in.

Like a prisoner.

The barely restrained anger marring Honey's handsome face as Mac dragged her from topside to below deck would forever be seared in her mind.

He was furious.

She knew he would be when he'd discovered her ruse.

She'd known he would be when he'd discovered her ruse. She understood his reaction. He felt like a fool, though that was never her intent. But she was still surprised to find herself locked away.

The metal clank of the key turning in the lock echoed in the emptiness of the room. Honey hadn't said a word as Mac walked away, carrying her to her new prison. Pain pierced her heart as if she'd been stabbed with a blade. With the back of her hand, she swiped at the lone tear rolling down her cheek. This wasn't how things were supposed to happen.

Everything had transpired so quickly. Too quickly.

One minute Storm was in front of her, and she was ready to confront him. And the next, he was calling her out. Making her identity known to Honey and the crew.

She'd learned enough about Honey in the time she'd spent with him to know that he thought people would see him as a dolt. How could he not know he had a woman onboard? She'd like to think it was because she'd done such a good job of hiding her true self, but she didn't think that was the case. There were times when she'd almost slipped. And times where Honey had looked at her funny. As if he knew something was amiss but couldn't quite put his finger on it.

The feelings she had for him had been growing deeper by the day.

Did he feel the same way? His crew wouldn't take kindly to that revelation.

The heaviness of that possibility being true draped her in a feeling of unease. If he felt anything for her, he couldn't say anything. He wouldn't even be able to admit to himself what he was feeling.

She looked around the room. It held a small table with a lantern and a plain wooden chair. Nothing else. She dropped into the chair, pondering what would happen next.

Would he throw her out to sea so she met her death in the depths of the water?

Make her walk the plank?

Run her through with his sword?

The only person that should be run through with a sword was Storm. He'd caused this whole situation.

Above her, she could hear conversations but could not make out the words. Night was beginning to fall, and she wondered what steps Honey would take to go after Storm. She knew that Honey wanted to cut him down almost as much as she did.

She hadn't realized how close Honey was to her father. Honey's name had been mentioned here and there in conversations, but her father was never one to offer information about his sea-faring dealings. Sean preferred to keep the specifics out of family conversations. That was his way of keeping them safe.

Seonag did take solace in the fact that she wasn't alone in knowing what an unsavory character Storm had turned out to be. She only wished her father had seen the scum for what he was before it was too late. The bastard would pay. If she weren't the one to mete out the justice her father so deserved, she was sure Honey would deal the final death blow.

The sound of footsteps caught her attention. She stood and focused on the door. The footsteps got closer and then passed. Her heart sank as they faded away. Seonag feared that she would be spending the night alone in this room. With no bed.

"'Tis fine," she murmured. "I can sleep on the floor." She'd essentially been doing that ever since boarding the *Hella*. Though in this room, no pallet was to be found. She wasn't really worried about that. Her concern was about what Honey was going to do. What punishment did he see fit for her deception?

She wished she'd had the chance to explain herself. To make him understand why she wanted to get to Storm herself. To let him know who she really was. Right now, he knew she wasn't Sean, but he didn't know *who* she was. He knew her real name. But she wanted Honey to know that she was Sean's daughter. She felt that piece was important.

Time dragged by as she waited for Honey to come to get her. She was exhausted but couldn't sleep. Honey's furious face kept flashing in her mind. It pained her even more to know that she was the cause.

Colin sat in his captain quarters, putting away a steady stream of whisky. "How could I have been so blind?" He spat the question out into the air of his empty room.

Peggy had offered his ear to talk, but Colin had declined. He didn't want to talk to anyone right now.

Sean—no, not Sean—had made a fool out of him. How would his men respect him now? What the hell was her name anyway? What had Storm said again? His mind was too muddled to remember. Who the hell was she, and what was her plan?

He thought back to the time they'd spent together. Those times where he found Sean's behavior odd for a lad. It all made sense now. They'd gotten close in these past few weeks during their time chasing Storm. She knew his darkest secrets. His greatest fears.

She also knew everything about him. His books. His finances. His holdings.

Jesus, he'd been taken for a fool.

She'd even had him questioning himself. He slammed his cup down on the table with such force he heard the wood crack. "That's why she didn't want to undress in front of my men or me. Damn it. If she did, we would have found out the truth."

She'd bested him, and that was unacceptable. Any trust that had grown between them was gone now.

If there was one thing Colin demanded, it was loyalty. How could she be loyal if she couldn't even trust him with her secret? Because there had to be a secret. What obvious reason could there be for her ruse? It had to be bad enough that she felt the need to be someone else.

But Storm had recognized her right away. Why? He didn't

seem surprised to see her on the *Hella* either. That proved they had a history.

Was she Storm's ex-lover? Had he left her, and she was trying to find him again?

Nay she accused Storm of killing him. *Killing who?*

He took another long swallow of whisky, cognizant of the fact that as much as he wanted to lose himself in his cups, he couldn't. He needed to remain alert. The *Revenge of Hades* was within firing distance. He wasn't ready to take that step yet, but he couldn't predict what Storm would do and he wanted to be prepared.

Peggy knocked on his door, opening it a crack and poking his head in. "Cap'n?" he asked warily.

"What do ye want, Peggy?"

"I thought I should check in on ye. See how ye're faring?"

"Hmph. Aside from being made a fool?"

"Och, Honey, I wouldna go that far."

Colin barked out a laugh. "Nay? Did ye put all yer trust into a lad only to find out he's a lass?"

"She must have a good reason, Honey. I know ye're upset now. Talk to the lass. Find out her intentions." Peggy grabbed a cup, poured himself a dram of whisky, and downed it in one swallow.

"Mayhap. Or mayhap she's a spy working for Storm sent to infiltrate our crew."

Peggy shook his head. "I dinna believe that to be the truth. And I dinna think ye believe that, either. Ye heard her accuse Storm of killing Sean."

Colin held out his cup, and Peggy filled it. He downed it in one swallow, and savored the burn as the liquid settled down deep into his chest. He dropped into the chair and sighed. "I'm not sure I can face the lass after her betrayal, Peggy."

"Honey, I know ye almost better than anyone. And I know ye dinna mean that."

He slammed his fist on the desk. "Damn it, man! I dinna know what to do." He wasn't lying. For once in his life, he didn't know how to proceed.

"Listen, sleep on it tonight. She's not going anywhere. Ye've locked her in that room. Talk to her in the morn. Listen to what she has to say. She might surprise ye."

He wasn't sure about that. But Peggy's advice was well taken. Sleep wouldn't come easy tonight, but mayhap he could help it along with more whisky.

Peggy left him to his vices, and with each sip Colin took, his anger began to subside a bit more.

CHAPTER 15

*S*eonag didn't know how much time had passed as she waited for Honey to see her. The ship was dark and silent as it sliced through the water, rocking the boat gently.

Knowing that Honey wouldn't appear to speak with her until the morning, she'd settled on the floor, her back against the wall, and tried not to worry too much about what he'd do to her once he returned. The gentle bobbing of the boat lulled her into a calm state.

She heard footsteps moments before light illuminated the floor beneath the bottom of the door. She scrambled to her feet, wiping her suddenly damp palms on her pants. Her heart pounded in her chest. He'd come for her much earlier than she'd expected. She wasn't sure what to make of that.

She listened as the key was inserted into the lock and then twisted, freeing the mechanism.

But it wasn't Honey standing on the other side of the door when it swung open.

Sweeney entered the small space, seeming much larger

and imposing than she'd noticed before in all her previous interactions with him.

"Ye're to come with me." He sneered, looking her up and down with disdain. "I've got orders to fetch ye."

She flinched at the chosen word. Fetch—like one would a dog. That word told her all she needed to know about what Honey thought of her now. It was even more telling than Honey sending Sweeney, of all people, to get her.

The way Sweeney leered at her made her uncomfortable. A shiver crept down her spine as he drew closer, and she saw the rope he carried.

He grabbed her wrists roughly and bound them together in front of her. That eliminated any hope she'd had that Honey would be willing to listen to her reasoning. Nay, she truly was a prisoner. What had she expected? He was a pirate. Second chances weren't something they was known for.

"Walk," Sweeney ordered as he pushed her ahead of him.

"Where are we going?" she asked.

He ignored her as he led her silently above deck. Near the railing, he took his lantern and swept it over the dark blue water. What was he searching for? "This way." He grabbed her arm with a piercing grip.

She winced at the pain. Something was wrong. A dark sense of foreboding spread through her as he commanded her to climb over the side.

"Say anything, and I'll slit yer throat without so much as a hesitation."

She gasped and looked to where he pointed. A small boat bobbed on the surface of the water. A figure waited there. Was it Honey? Was Honey going to bring her out to sea and toss her in the water? Could he really be so cruel? She hadn't thought so. Mayhap she didn't know him as well as she thought.

Her stomach sank, and she started to shake.

"Go on," he urged, his eyes darting around nervously.

She lifted her leg cautiously over the side, her foot searching for the rope ladder. She prayed her body didn't betray her and send her hurtling into the cold water. She was terrified of falling. When she was sure of her footing, she swung her other leg down, her hands grasping onto the rough rope in a death grip. Slowly, she climbed down the ladder, getting closer to the boat and the waiting figure below with every step. Not an easy task, especially with her wrists still bound. She was forced to keep them near to her chest and maneuver carefully to ensure she didn't lose her footing and splash into the sea below.

Sweeney was right above her. "Move faster," he demanded in a harsh whisper.

The rope bit into the palms of her hands as she slid along the ladder, careful to keep her balance.

Before she even reached the bottom rung, the figure in the boat grasped her around the waist and pulled her down into the boat. She let out a yelp and looked at the man.

It wasn't Honey. The man was familiar, but his name slipped past her memory. He was one of her father's old crew members. Her heart dropped.

That could mean only one thing. She was being brought to Storm.

Sweeney dropped into the boat and sat in front of her.

"Why are ye doing this? Honey will have yer head fer this." She warned.

Sweeney scoffed at her words. "Have ye no' spoken to him recently? He wants nothing to do with ye after yer betrayal."

"Then why the secrecy? Why take me away under cover of darkness?"

She saw the fear cross over his face in the faint light of

the lantern hanging at the side of the boat. There it was—Honey didn't know she was being taken. She opened her mouth to scream out to him but swiftly, Sweeney clasped a hand over it.

"Make any noise, and I swear to ye, I'll cut yer pretty little throat and throw ye to the sharks."

She felt cold steel against the skin of her neck and stiffened. His eyes were pure evil as he spat the words, his vile spittle spraying her face. She did not doubt that he was telling the truth.

Tears threatened, but she needed to stay strong. Now was not the time to cry. She refused to show him any weakness.

Seonag's mind raced as she grappled to come up with a plan that would get her back to the *Hella* and Honey.

The full moon lit the night, and its reflection bounced along the surface of the water. With each stroke of the oars, they got closer and closer to the *Revenge of Hades* and her father's killer. This was what she had wanted from the first time she'd decided to make Storm pay. It was the whole reason for her dressing as Sean and hoping to fool Honey and the rest of his crew.

Now she was being delivered to Storm on a platter. She thought of the small dagger tucked into her boot that Peggy had handed to her. Imagined the satisfaction she would feel if given a chance to sink the cold blade deep into Storm's black heart.

"What are ye smiling about?" Sweeney asked.

She hadn't realized she'd let her feelings show. She glared at her captor across from her, and behind him, the looming form of the *Revenge of Hades* appeared.

What was Storm's plan? Yes, he'd recognized her, but what did that mean? He had her father's ship. Was the self-proclaimed captain of his crew. According to Honey, he also had the gold coins her father was transporting. What more could he possibly want? The thought of everything he had made her seethe. Shake with anger. He'd never worked for anything a day in his life. Her father had felt pity for him. Offered him a position in his crew because he wanted to give him a chance. In doing so, her father had unknowingly signed his death warrant.

Her fists clenched in her lap. They coasted to a stop at the side of the ship, where men were waiting to bring them aboard.

Sweeney pulled her brutishly to her feet and shoved her toward one of the waiting men. The man unceremoniously threw her over his shoulder and climbed up the ladder, uncouthly depositing her on the deck.

She stumbled and almost fell before she found her balance and straightened. Storm stood in front of her, his fingers hooked in the belt loops of his trews. His dark eyes bore into hers.

Though she was scared to death and trembling inside, she refused to look away. Refused to show him how frightened she was. Silently in her head, she kept repeating to herself, "stay strong. Stay strong."

"Seonag. 'Tis been a while since last we've seen each other." He dropped his eyes to her booted feet and slowly drew them up her body until he met her eyes once again. He sneered. "My condolences on your da. I'm sure it was a difficult time for ye and yer mother."

How dare he? She launched herself at him. He was lucky her hands were still bound. She would have gouged his eyeballs out if they weren't.

Sweeney caught her around the waist and held her in place as Storm threw his head back and laughed.

"Honey must be both daft and blind if he truly believed ye were a lad." He stepped closer and trailed a rough, calloused finger down her jawline. "I'd never make that mistake."

She pulled away from his touch, but that just put her flush against Sweeney's chest. With her chin held high, she warned, "Dinna talk about him that way." Her voice came out as a low growl.

With a raised brow, he assessed her once more. "If I didna ken any better, I'd think ye are soft on the knave." He set his attention on Sweeney. "Ye proved yer loyalty. Welcome to the *Revenge of Hades*."

"Thank ye, Cap'n," Sweeney said as he made his way around Seonag.

As he passed Storm, the captain reached out and ran a blade across the man's throat.

Sweeney clasped his hands to his neck, eyes round in surprise as he tried to stop the flow of blood. He staggered to the boat rail, his face pale.

"Ye served yer purpose." Storm approached and kicked him square in the chest, sending his body overboard to crash into the water below.

He leered at Seonag. "Now, where were we? Oh, aye." He stalked toward her, grasping her arm so tightly it felt as if his fingertips were penetrating her skin, and dragged her forward. "Ye are coming with me. Set sail!" he ordered over his shoulder as he pulled her along behind him.

Planting her feet on the ground, she tried to put an end to him from forcing her to follow him, but she was no match for his brute strength. "Stop. Stop!"

Storm halted his procession.

"Where are ye bringing me?"

He grabbed her arm and yanked her along. "Ye'll see soon enough."

On their way to wherever Storm was leading her to, they passed crewmen who hooted and hollered. Vile phrases were thrown at her as if she were a whore. Traitors—the whole lot of them. She'd see each of them hanged.

Down the stairs, they went until they reached a familiar door. Her father's quarters. No. No longer her father's. Now they were Storm's.

He pushed her into the room and onto the bed, and she sprung up faster than even she knew she was capable of.

"Give me yer wrists." He reached for her with his free hand. In the other hand, he held a large dagger.

She did as she was told, leery as he cut the rope, then rubbed her wrists together. Her skin was bruised and chafed.

He pulled the chair out from the desk and pointed to it. "Since ye dinna want to sit on the bed, sit here."

"What do ye want, Storm?"

He leaned against the door frame and faced her. "Information."

That was not the answer she'd expected. It puzzled her. She shrugged. "I'm sorry. It appears ye've gone to a lot of trouble for naught."

"Dinna lie to me. Ye know Honey's plans. And his books."

She shook her head in denial, but he pierced her with an icy gaze. "Mayhap ye've forgotten how I got ye on this ship? Sweeney, disloyal vermin that he is—" He snickered and shook his head. "Correction, that he was, informed us of the role ye were playing on the *Hella*. Ye read his books. Know his numbers. What are they?"

That was what this was about? He wanted to know how much gold Honey possessed? Didn't he have enough of his own with the coin he'd stolen from her father when he killed him? Greedy bastard. It didn't matter. She would not reveal Honey's business to someone that had no right to know.

She concentrated on the rocking of the ship. She'd thought Storm would want to make haste and get to whatever destination he was going to as soon as possible, but the gentle sway of the boat as she sat watching Storm's every move suggested otherwise.

"Now is no time to be mute, Seonag. Tell me what ye know," he ordered, with an edge to his tone that sent chills down her spine.

He had killed her father. None of his actions up to this point made her think he wouldn't do the same to her. Her only hope would be to delay until she could plunge her dagger into him or Honey and his crew attacked.

She might have deceived Honey, but he had to understand it was for a good reason. And now that reason had come to fruition. Her dagger burned in her boot, but Storm was watching her closely. If she had any chance of taking him down, she would need the element of surprise on her side.

"I dinna know how much he's worth, Storm," she lied. He wouldn't kill her until he had the information he was after. She needed to lead him along and bide her time.

CHAPTER 16

*I*n his quarters, Colin sat at his desk, a cask of whisky and a cup his only company. As much as he wanted to forget the woman locked in one of the rooms below, he couldn't stop thinking about her. He was constantly dismissing the urge to barge into her room and force her to open up to him.

He wanted to see her as the beautiful woman she really was.

But he needed answers first. His trust had been broken, and he didn't take lightly to that. He downed another dram of whisky, savoring the burn.

His desire would need to wait until morning at least. At first light, they needed to attack. It pained him to think he would be causing damage to the ship his friend had loved so much. But Storm wouldn't surrender. No pirate worth their weight in salt would. He understood that.

Unfortunately, that meant the *Revenge of Hades* would feel the wrath of his cannons. He only hoped Sean would understand. If Sean were in his shoes, Colin would expect him to stop at nothing to avenge his name and legacy.

Standing, he stretched and cracked his back. He wanted to meet up with his men and go over the plans for the morning. In the hall, he paused by the door he'd had Mac lock Sean—he couldn't remember what her name was—in. A twinge of guilt pierced his gut. He leaned against the door, listening. She made no sound. She must've fallen asleep.

Fighting the temptation to unlock the door and let her out, he kept walking, trying to focus on what he needed to do.

"Ye need anything, Cap'n?" Duncan asked as he made his way past him topside.

"Nay, just this eternal night to end," Colin answered.

He had to find Peggy. His quartermaster was seated at a table with another crew member, playing a game of draughts with the board set up between them.

"Who's winning?" Colin asked as he pulled up a chair and sat down, stretching his long legs in front of him.

"Peggy, of course," Derrick said. "The bastard always cheats." He grabbed an empty cup, poured some ale into it, and handed it to Colin while Peggy thought about his next move.

"Ah, shut up, ye son of a strumpet." He moved his wooden coin, jumping over two of Derrick's coins, and proclaimed, "King me."

Derrick threw up his hands. "I give up."

"Come on. Ye'll never learn if ye always quit before the end."

Honey laughed as he watched the exchange between the two men. Peggy older, Derrick younger. He nodded at Derrick, one of his newer crewmen. "Ye should take lessons from ol' Peggy here. There's wisdom in his strategy. Which, speaking of..." He looked at his quartermaster. "We need to discuss our approach for the morn and get everything ready."

"Aye, Cap'n." He stood and turned to Derrick. "Put the

board up and then gather the rest of the crew. Meet us above deck after a bit."

～

Two hours later, Colin and his crew had a plan of attack. The mutinous crew of the *Revenge of Hades* would pay, but especially Storm. He wanted to rip that louse apart limb by limb. He was all for aiming the cannons now and blowing the ship to pieces.

Damn him and his honor. He'd always gone by the edict that he wouldn't fire upon his enemy under cover of darkness. He knew he was alone in his thinking. Most pirates in his situation wouldn't blink an eye. They'd attack whenever given the chance.

Colin made up his own rules and stuck by them. Even when his crew disagreed. But they knew the rules before they signed on. If they didn't like it, they didn't have to work for him. There were plenty of other captains out there looking for help.

But make no mistake, just because he waited for the light of day, he held nothing back. Took no mercy on those he attacked. The best part about carrying his plans through when he did?

He got to see the life seep out of the eyes of his enemies as they died by his hand.

～

Shortly before dawn broke the night sky, Colin got out of bed. He hadn't slept anyway. His eyes continuously fell upon the empty pallet on the floor near his bed.

Guilt flooded him as he thought about how he'd made a lass sleep on his floor. Worse, he'd undressed in front of her.

She'd seen him. All of him. 'Twas no wonder she always shied away from him during those times. He was a fool.

"Cap'n!" Peggy burst through the door, his round face red, his barrel chest heaving. "The *Revenge of Hades*. It's gone."

"What are ye going on about?" He bent over the wash-basin and splashed his face with the cool water, running his wet hands through his hair before taking a strip of linen and tying it at his nape.

"Storm has pulled anchor and gone. The ship. It's not there. I've no idea when he left."

"Coward. He was still anchored when we were planning our attack. That means he could only have a few hours on us at the most." He pushed past his quartermaster and headed topside. He looked over the water. Dawn was just cresting, the morn still dark, but light enough for him to see there were no other ships around them.

"Damn it!" he swore. The air was stagnant. "There's nay wind. The *Revenge of Hades* will be becalmed in this weather. Call up the others and set sail."

The *Hella* was a larger ship with more force behind it to coast along the sea's surface. He had no doubt they'd catch the traitorous bastards before long.

"Aye, Cap'n. Which direction?"

"North. Storm will be heading past Aberdeen. He's got allies out that way. If he was looking for someone to put him up so he and his crew could lay low for a while, that's where he'd go."

Peggy nodded and went to gather the men. Colin remained on deck, a feeling of disappointment gnawing at his gut. He'd been anticipating a battle. If Storm thought he'd escaped his wrath, he was dead wrong.

Colin would get the battle he sought.

CHAPTER 17

*S*eonag was growing tired of being locked in rooms by men who thought they could dictate her every move.

She didn't understand why Storm thought she would provide him with the information he asked for. They'd never really gotten along. If he had any brains in that thick head of his, he'd know that she wouldn't do anything to assist him after he'd killed her father.

Beautiful blue eyes pierced her memory. A handsome face with a dimple that played peek-a-boo and only showed when he smiled a certain way. She prayed that she got the chance to explain, but right now, she needed to get the tempting pirate out of her thoughts.

She paced the room. Her dagger remained tucked in her boot. In that, she couldn't believe her luck. The room she was in was familiar. She'd been in it many times before. It was where she would always spend her time as a child when the ship was docked near home. Her mother had hated that her father took her on board, but she loved every minute of it.

It also confirmed Storm didn't know her at all.

God had heard her prayers by placing her in this room, her father's old study of sorts while he was at sea. And while the room brought back painful memories and reminded her that she would never see her father again, it also held pleasant memories. Seonag, sitting on Sean's lap as he told her tall tales of sea monsters.

It was also the room where he'd kept a small box of treasures. In that box was an extra key to this room.

Had Storm found that small box and removed it?

She listened for the sound of anyone near, and when she heard nothing, she went over to the far wall. A tapestry of a bird in a gilded cage hung there, flanked by two wall sconces. To the casual observer, they looked exactly the same with nothing hidden in their depths.

And that was the idea.

She approached the left sconce and tentatively slid it to the right. Behind it was a hollowed-out space in the wall. She reached in, her fingertips skimming the surface of the box, and with a sigh of relief pulled out the small, covered chest hidden inside.

Storm hadn't found it. He probably didn't know the treasure existed.

Carefully sliding the sconce back in place, she walked to the door and held her breath, listening again for any movement outside.

Dead silence greeted her ears, and she was thankful once again. Her good fortune could only be attributed to her father's spirit. This was him watching over her. She could feel his presence all around her, and she whispered a quick prayer of thanks.

Lifting the cover of the box, she studied the contents. It had been a while since she'd seen them. Years, actually. She grabbed the key and shoved it into her pocket. The other items weren't worth anything monetarily but held plenty of sentimental value. Small shells she'd collected from walking the shore with her father, their bare feet sinking into the wet sand.

Her heart ached as her fingers ran over the shells' surfaces. Some were smooth, some rough.

"I promise ye that Storm will pay for all he's done to ye and our family." A lone tear left a thin trail of wetness on her cheek as it wound its way down her face until finally falling off her jawline and onto her hand.

The *Revenge of Hades* loomed ahead in the distance, slowly limping along in the water in front of them.

"The coward was tryin' to outrun ye, Cap'n," Peggy remarked.

"Aye."

"Looks as if the knave underestimated the wind and the quickness of his ship."

Colin couldn't hide his smile at the thoughtless fool. "Ready the cannons," he yelled.

A chorus of "Aye, Cap'n!" answered him.

He studied his men. "Where's Sweeney?"

Mac looked around. "I dinna see him, Cap'n."

A sinking feeling settled into the pit of his stomach. "Go check on the lass."

Mac dipped his head and headed below deck.

If Sweeney harmed one hair on the the lass's head, he'd flay the cretin before using him as bait. His reaction shook him to his core. The realization that his feelings ran deeper than friendship dawned on him and for a moment he forgot about her deceit.

Worry for her safety seeped into his veins.

He kept an eye on their target while he impatiently waited for Mac to return.

A few minutes later, Mac scrambled up the stairs. "Cap'n. She's gone. I've searched everywhere below deck. She's no' on the *Hella*. Neither is Sweeney."

Now he knew why Storm had fled during the night.

"Sweeney must have handed her over to Storm." He refused to believe that she went willingly. He knew she wasn't fond of Sweeney. The deckhand was constantly harassing her.

But why would Sweeney commit such a betrayal?

Colin hadn't had time to question the lass on what she and Storm's relationship was. "Watch for the lass when we attack."

They drew nearer, the distance between the two ships growing smaller. They were well within the range of a clear shot. Colin wanted to make sure the heathens could see what was coming.

"Ready. Hold." He waited until they were perfectly aligned. "Fire!" His ears rang as the cannons flew through the air, crashing through the wooden sides of the *Revenge of Hades*.

The screams of men carried on the wind as they scattered, some falling over the side into the water.

His crew was lined up at the rails. Ready to cross over and board the other ship. Colin stood with them, his hand on his sword. Anticipation thrummed through him at the thought of piercing Storm's heart with the tip of his blade. He'd stare him straight in the eye as he took his life. And the bastard would know why he was doing it.

In the name of Sean, Colin would avenge all the wrongs done to him and his family.

The two ships were so close to each other. Peggy maneuvered the *Hella* with the expertise worthy of a captain.

"Lay the planks," Honey commanded as his crew hurried to make a bridge between the two ships, and then scrambled across. "Take no quarter!" He yelled and followed his men onboard the *Revenge of Hades*.

He ducked the blade of an enemy and sank his sword into the man's gut. His cry of agony was a beautiful song to Colin's ears. He slashed his way dockside. He needed to find Storm. And the lass. The coward wasn't fighting with his men on the front lines. He had to be hiding below deck.

Colin would find him. "Storm is mine," he called. "If ye find him, bring him to me. Dinna hurt the lass when ye find her."

CHAPTER 18

A sudden boom rocked the ship and the box shot from Seonag's hands as she was knocked to the floor. The whole room shook around her, splinters of wood falling from the ceiling all around her.

They were under attack. Had Honey come for her? *Did he even know she was gone?*

She scrambled to her feet and fumbled around in her pocket for the key to the door. She'd be damned if the ship was going down with her locked in this room. Jabbing the key into the slot, she said a quick prayer and turned her wrist, and thanked the Lord above when she heard the click and was able to open the door.

Running at full speed, she took off down the hall and ran right into the hard chest of Storm.

He caught hold of her arm. "Where do ye think ye're going?" His hot, fetid breath assaulted her face. He dragged her behind him, her shorter legs no match for his long strides. She kept losing her footing, which only angered him more.

"Let go of me, ye knave," Seonag yelled. She tried yanking

her arm out of his grasp, but it was of no use. He was too strong for her.

He halted in his tracks and pulled her body up close to his, their faces mere inches away from one another. "Stop fighting me," he demanded.

She formed her free hand into a claw and swiped at his face. Satisfaction warmed her soul when she made contact and he pushed her away with a curse.

But not for long. "Ye bitch." He swung out and slapped her cheek, the smack startling her before he grasped her arm once again and hauled her forward.

"Ye killed my father."

He drew up short and looked her in the eye. "Aye, I did. The bastard wanted to be honorable and not keep all the gold he was transporting. The gold is enough to fund our endeavors for many months to come. He was a fool not to want to keep it for himself."

"He wasna a fool. My father was an honorable man."

"He was a pirate. He was stupid to think he could do the right thing. That's no' what we're aboot."

Storm began to move forward again, tugging her along behind him. She tried to reach down into her boot and retrieve the dagger Peggy had given her earlier. At the time, she'd had no idea she would be put in this situation. But as she stumbled along, she knew in her heart it was the right time.

This was her time.

Seonag would make her father proud. Her fingers closed around the hilt of the dagger, and she pulled it out, careful not to lose her grasp. Storm wasn't paying any attention to her. He was concentrating on getting them to wherever he was bringing her.

She raised her arm and, with all her strength, thrust it into the center of Storm's back.

He dropped her arm and staggered back, reaching for the blade that was now protruding from his back, a shocked look upon his face.

"Ye feckin' b—" He stumbled to his knees before he could finish his sentence, before falling face down on the floor.

Seonag didn't wait to see if he still breathed. She ran topside so that she could cross back over to the *Hella*. As much as she loved her father's ship, right now, she just wanted off of it.

As she ran, she sent a quick prayer up to her father and whispered, "I did it, Da."

~

As Colin slashed his way onto the *Revenge of Hades* he couldn't help but search for the lass. He now stood topside, his men making easy work of the traitorous crew, but he still hadn't seen Storm.

Or the lass.

What type of captain didn't fight with his crew?

A cowardly one. Colin answered his own question. Storm didn't have one lick of integrity running through his cold veins.

He ducked the swing of a sword from one of Storm's men. The man stumbled forward and Colin turned, blade out, the metal slicing through the man's gut. He let out a cry before crumbling to the floor.

Colin looked from side to side. Trying to keep his attention on the fight at hand, but also looking for the lass, he crept closer to the stairs that would lead him below deck. He hadn't seen her or Storm since he came onboard.

She had to be safe. He refused to accept any other scenario. But he had to find her. The longer she stayed out of his sight, the higher the chance that she could be harmed.

Because Storm was an untrustworthy cad.

At this point, Colin didn't care what the reason for the lass's deception was. He wanted her unharmed. The thought of her being anything but was almost unbearable.

And that was when he knew the realization slammed into his stomach like a fist.

This feeling swirling within him.

He was in love with the lass—and he didn't even know her name.

Colin looked around. His men had the mutinous crew under control. Most had been cut down and the few that remained were fighting losing battles with his much stronger men.

With the fight all but over, Storm's cowardly ways were on full display. He hadn't even appeared to fight with his men. What kind of captain backed away from a fight his men were giving their lives for?

"Honey," a feminine voice called to him from the stairs leading to the quarters below.

He turned and saw the lass he'd been searching for, blood on the front of her tunic.

She was alive…but wounded?

He rushed to her. "Lass, are ye alright?"

Her blue eyes round with fear as she took in the sight around her, she nodded her head.

Relief flooded over him.

He swept her up in his arms and captured her mouth with his. Her warm lips softened to his and it took all of his strength to break the kiss.

Wisps of hair had escaped her cap and curled around her face. A face that he would like to study further, but now wasn't the time.

"St-st-storm," she stuttered as he sat her on her feet.

"Where is he?"

The lass pointed to the stairs.

Colin ran over, descending them two at a time, until he was below deck. It was eerily quiet down here. He could hear the creaking of the ship as it bobbed along the sea.

He heard a moan and headed in the direction where he thought the sound came from. Before he located the source, he found a pool of blood. It smeared across the floor as if something had been dragged through it.

He followed the trail and before long, Storm was in front of him, crawling on the floor.

Colin saw the blade protruding from his back. He recognized it as one that Peggy had carried.

The same one the man had given to the lass. A burst of pride swelled his chest.

She did this.

The lass was a fighter. And had managed to take down Storm. Not completely, but nearly so. It was only a matter of time until he succumbed to his wounds.

Colin approached the cretin. Placing his boot on the man's lower back, he bent down and pulled the dagger out of Storm's torso, wiping the blood on his trews before tucking the blade in his boot.

Ignoring his curse, Colin took Storm by the shoulders and turned him over so they could look at each other face to face.

Even on the brink of death, the bastard sneered at him.

"What are ye waiting for? Or has not being able to tell a lad from a lass taken away yer fight?"

In an instant, Colin had the tip of his sword at Storm's throat. "Mayhap, I want to watch as yer life slowly ebbs into nothingness."

Storm chuckled, the action causing him to cough, and Colin's sword pierced the skin of Storm's neck. A thin trickle of blood trailed out of the cut.

"What did ye do to her?"

"No' a thing. The lass was locked in a room when ye attacked." He coughed and drops of blood dripped from his mouth. "The wench caught me unawares."

"Too bad she didna finish ye off." He pressed his sword deeper into Storm's neck. "That is what I'm here for. Ye killed Sean. Left his family bereft and poverty stricken. This is for him. And for them."

Colin stabbed his sword deep into Storm's neck and watched as the man's eyes widened before the life seeped out of them.

He retrieved his sword and placed it back in its scabbard.

"Ye have been avenged, my friend. May ye rest in peace now." Colin looked up to the heavens and took a deep breath. He knew Sean was proud of him.

CHAPTER 19

The lass he'd known as Sean had opted to stay on the *Revenge of Hades* while his men sent her father's traitorous crew to their watery graves. Was it a coincidence that her name was the same as the friend he'd just avenged? Colin didn't think so. Especially when he saw the way she longingly looked at his friend's ship.

Now that the dirty work was done, she would join him on the *Hella* for the sail back home.

Colin was both furious and relieved as he waited for the lass to board the *Hella*.

Furious that he didn't know the truth yet.

Relieved that she wasn't hurt.

He stood, shoulders back, arms crossed with his mouth in a firm line. He was sure he looked like a mad bastard, but he didn't care.

He was.

The worry and concern he'd felt these past hours were nearly unbearable, and he wasn't happy about it. He hadn't been that worried for as long as he could remember.

And he didn't want to be in a situation like that again, ever.

As she traversed the planks between the two ships and stepped onto the deck, Colin moved forward and was instantly blocked by every single member of his crew. They formed a line, a barrier of sorts, between him and the lass.

"What the hell do ye think ye are doing?"

Peggy took a position at the front of the men. "Protecting the lass."

"Are ye daft, man?"

Peggy folded his beefy arms across his chest, feet wide apart, mimicking Colin's stance from earlier. "Mayhap. What are yer plans?"

"Lest ye not forget who ye are talking to, Old Salt." The statement was funny. The man was far from old, but Colin had no patience left. "I'm still the captain of this ship."

"Och, aye. I ken that, *Captain*," he said snidely. "But the lass has done naught wrong. If ye plan to harm her, I'll stop ye. Captain or no."

"Aye," came the echo from the others flanked behind Peggy.

Colin raised a brow in challenge. "Will ye now? What has the lass done for ye? Ye dinna even ken who she is."

Peggy hunched his shoulders in a shrug. "I ken who she is fine. She's been kind and caring to the whole crew. Even when she posed as a lad, she's been naught but helpful. Look how carefully she stitched up Duncan. She provided us meals that were worth eating. Mended our tunics and trews."

Peggy paused and lowered his voice. "Think on all she did for ye. She didna deserve to be turned over to that bastard, Storm. Ye havena any idea what ordeal she may have gone through while under his lock and key."

Colin knew Peggy was right. She'd had her reason for

doing what she did. And his feelings were muddled between being angry at her for her betrayal and wanting to sweep her into his arms again and kiss away all her fears. But he couldn't tell his crew that. "Hmph, she was naught but dishonest. Lying about who she really was," Colin said unconvincingly.

He had no idea how she'd grown such a strong support system, but apparently, she had his crew under her thumb. He regarded his men and looked each one of them in the eye. Not one of them bent under his scrutiny. They stood their ground and held his gaze.

The lass had proven helpful, and listening to Peggy admit to that was quite the feat. Women weren't welcome onboard. For his crew to step up and say they were willing to allow it said more than any words they could ever voice aloud.

And the twinge of excitement Colin felt at finding out the lad was a lass, was something he could not ignore. The unexplained pull he'd had toward her since the first time he'd unknowingly laid eyes on her made sense now, though it didn't at the time.

"I'm no' going to harm the lass, Peggy. Ye can be certain of that."

His quartermaster looked at him as if he'd grown two heads. "Ye give yer word?"

Colin was irritated at being questioned, but he nodded in acquiescence. "Aye. Ye know me better than that, Peggy. I've yet to harm a lass. Innocent or no'."

Peggy nodded, then smiled. "I knew ye'd come around to see things the right way."

"I'm still going to talk to the lass," Colin said. "I've a right to know why she needled her way onto my ship." He grinned at his play on words.

The *Hella* rocked gently, and when his crew parted, the lass stood in the opening created by the men. Her cheeks pink, her blue eyes round and wide, as she stayed rooted in that place and assessed him warily.

He knew his men were watching his every move. They should all know that he wouldn't hurt the lass. He looked beyond her, and out in the water past her shoulder, at the *Revenge of Hades* as it bobbed along the water. It had sustained some heavy damage from the cannons, but it remained afloat and sailable. They would take her back to Lunan Bay with them.

"We have things we must discuss." He aimed his words at the lass, and she brought her eyes up to meet his. "My quarters."

"Cap'n," Peggy stepped forward, but the lass stopped him with a gentle hand on his arm.

Colin wanted to feel those small fingers touching his own arm.

"'Tis fine, Peggy." She gave a small smile to the man standing up for her. "Yer captain willna hurt me." She moved past Peggy and around Duncan and continued past Colin, her head held high, and headed in the direction of his quarters.

Colin turned on his heel and followed. He had the feeling the upcoming conversation would be one of the most enlightening he'd ever been privy to.

CHAPTER 20

In Honey's captain's quarters, all Seonag wanted to do was breathe a sigh of relief. Well, mayhap she wanted to run into his muscular arms and have their strength envelop her, too. She was tough, but she wished for his support at the moment.

His blond brows furrowed together as he studied her, making her feel self-conscious. She worried her lower lip with her teeth as her nerves took her on a journey of anxiety she had no interest in taking.

"Sit," he commanded.

She did so without hesitation. Uneasy anticipation made her plop on the bed unceremoniously. She watched him quietly as he drew near and stopped in front of her, making her tilt her head up so she could look him in his eyes. Beautiful blue eyes that were currently shadowed.

In concern?

Anger?

His legs were in such proximity to her knees that she could feel the warmth of his body through the material of the trews she wore.

"Honey, I —"

"I din—"

They started speaking at the same time and both paused. Honey clamped his mouth shut, his full lips forming a thin line. He was upset with her. She couldn't blame him. For a man who demanded trust and loyalty above all else, her deception these past few weeks had to have hit him as a punch in the gut.

Perhaps he would throw her overboard. But deep in her heart, she knew he would never do that.

He'd kissed her with such emotion earlier, she blushed thinking about it now.

He was a good man. It wasn't in his nature to intentionally hurt a lass, though she was sure the thought must have crossed his mind a time or two. But his crew didn't feel the same way. They'd stood up for her before Honey had agreed he wouldn't harm her.

That gesture had to mean something. She'd somehow managed to win favor with them. Now, if she could only do the same with the intimidating pirate standing so close to her.

Honey remained silent. His eyes were searching her face. Was he waiting for her to continue?

She cleared her throat nervously. Her tongue felt thick in her mouth as she pondered what to say. "First, I would like to apologize."

He scoffed loudly, rolling his eyes to the sky, but said nothing.

"My actions were selfish."

"Ye could have been killed," he boomed. "Are ye daft?"

She shrunk back at the anger in his words. His temper caused his nostrils to flare and his eyes to darken even more.

Noticing her reaction, he put his hands up and stepped away from her, adding some distance between them as he leaned against the wooden desk and crossed his legs at the ankles. The worn leather of his boots was faded in some spots.

"I'm no' fond of being made a fool of in front of my men." He pierced her with an icy gaze. "I've made men walk the plank for less."

Seonag swallowed hard, forcing away the lump in her throat so she could speak. "Other than my name, I've been truthful with ye."

"How about posing as a lad?"

She blew out a breath. "Aye, that, too. But nothing else."

"Yer age?"

Seonag threw her hands up in frustration. "Oh, alright, ye've got me there as well."

"Is that all?"

"Fine, but there's one more thing. And truly, this is the last. My mother is alive. 'Tis only my father that is no longer with us." Her breath hitched at the mention of Sean.

She'd done this all for him.

Honey's brows knitted together, but he remained quiet.

"For months, I've been waiting for Storm to come to our shores."

Honey slammed his hand down on the flat top of his desk. "I knew ye were intimate with the bastard."

"No! Absolutely not." The man was exasperating.

"How about ye begin from the beginning? Yer true name for a start." Even though he knew it already, he must want to hear it from her lips.

She stalled, picking at an invisible piece of lint on her trews. "Seonag," she said quietly.

"What was that?" Honey asked, leaning closer to hear her better.

"My name is Seonag. My father was Captain Sean Ruane."

~

Colin flinched at what he'd just heard. The lass was his friend's daughter? He thought back to their time spent on the ship. It all made sense. Her odd behavior. The way she'd taken a keen interest in any topic revolving around Storm or the *Revenge of Hades*.

"My father was killed this past year."

"Aye. I ken."

She stood, rubbing her damp palms on her thighs, and paced the small space between them. "That's why I was waiting for Storm to show his traitorous face."

Colin knew where she was going with her thoughts. But he gave her the space he felt she needed to tell her story. She didn't need any assistance from him.

"Storm killed my father. He told my mother and me that Da was killed by the Spanish fleet after an attack. I've been watching that shoreline every day since I found out I'd never see Da again." She drew in a deep, shuddering breath before continuing. "Once I saw that Da was the only one who perished in the attack and that the *Revenge of Hades* was in almost the same condition as when they'd set sail for that voyage, I knew Storm was behind his death.

"The Spaniards are cruel. The crew and ship would have never made it back to shore if they'd truly been ambushed, as Storm claimed. I swore I would make him pay for his sins. When I was in that pub and heard ye were going after him, I knew I needed to be on your ship."

Round, blue eyes met his, wet with unshed tears. A silent plea swam in their depths.

"Why lie? Why no' just ask me?"

The look she gave him told him she knew as well as he did that if she'd approached him as a lass and asked the same, he'd have turned her around so quickly, that she wouldn't have had time to voice a protest.

"Ye know the answer to that question. Ye're a smart man, Honey. Dinna make me spell it out for ye." She looked him dead in the eye and proclaimed, "Storm was mine to kill."

The fervor in which she made that statement shocked him. If he didn't know any better, he'd think she was one of his men, battle-hardened with multiple kills under her belt. He understood her motive for doing what she'd done.

Sean had talked lovingly about his family whenever they'd gathered together in an inn somewhere. Serving wenches had hung all over the two of them, even though Sean kindly fought off their advances and denied their offerings. He'd always remained true and faithful to his wife, wanting to offer her a better life than the one she'd entered into at their marriage ceremony.

Colin scratched his chin, the few days of stubble itchy under his fingers. "It seems we had a common goal. We both wanted to see Storm pay for his transgressions."

She nodded but didn't utter a word, even as he stood and approached her. The way she worried her lower bottom lip between her teeth made it plump and pink. And inviting. He had the urge to suck it into his mouth. To once again taste the sweetness that he knew was inside that luscious mouth. She met his eyes, unspoken emotions clouding their blue depths.

He plucked the cap off her head, revealing the hair she'd carefully pinned to hide it from him and the others. Slowly, Colin pulled each pin out, watching in wonderment as the curls fell not quite to her shoulders. Her hair was shorter than most women's. An unfortunate outcome of posing as a lad.

"Yer hair," he whispered, smoothing it with shaking hands. "Did ye shear it for this?"

Absently, she brought her hand up and twirled a chestnut-colored tendril around her fingers. "Aye. 'Twas easier to hide under my cap that way."

He continued stroking her hair. Couldn't stop himself from doing so. His groin tightened at the close contact and the silk of her tresses sliding between his fingers. The heat of her body, so near to his, seeped through his trews. "I'm sorry ye felt ye couldna be forthcoming to me about who ye really were." He grasped her hand, so wee in size compared to his own, and stroked the soft skin with his fingers. "But I understand yer reasoning."

Before he could think about what he was doing, he brought her hand up and placed his lips on her fingers, giving them a soft kiss.

She sucked in a sharp intake of breath and immediately pulled away. Dropping her hand, he stood and walked to the other side of the room, purposely putting distance between them. "I'm sorry, lass."

Colin should leave. If he had one honorable bone in his body, he would open the door in front of him and walk away. But he was feeling anything but honorable. His thoughts were even less so.

She approached him apprehensively, and took his large hands into her tiny ones, and gazed into his eyes. The stormy clouds in hers hit him right in the gut.

"I know I've been deceptive." She placed a small hand on his chest.

He tilted his head back and savored the warmth spreading across his skin, even through his tunic.

"It wasna to hurt ye. I needed to avenge my father's death, and ye were the means to that end." She buried her face into his chest, and he couldn't help but wrap his arms around her. She was so tiny against him.

"The feelings that we've both been fighting for weeks are real. Ye canna deny them," she whispered.

She looked up at him, pleading in her eyes, and he knew she was right.

He brought his head down, and to his delight, she tilted her chin up to him, allowing him access to her lips. With fervor, he captured her mouth with his. His tongue ran along her teeth, seeking entry into her mouth. He sighed and pulled her closer when she obliged.

Bending, he scooped her legs up and cradled her in his arms as he carried her over to his bed and laid her down before him.

She sat up on her elbows, expectation clear on her pretty face. Her bright blue eyes contrasted against her chestnut hair, giving her an ethereal beauty that Colin wanted to drown in. She was beautiful. He reached out and slowly ran his hands through her hair. "Ye need to let yer hair grow out again."

She nodded, but said nothing.

He nuzzled her neck. "I want ye, lass. I've wanted ye since almost the moment ye boarded my ship, much to my conflicted soul."

Seonag laughed, a deep throaty laugh, and he marveled at the seductive sound. She grasped his face and brought his lips down to meet hers in another scorching kiss.

She backed away, and pierced him with her sky-blue gaze. "I want ye, too, Colin Harris."

She didn't have to tell him twice. He gently nipped her neck and then brought his lips to her ear, sucking the lobe into his mouth. Her moan went straight to his groin, and his cock strained against his trews, wanting to break free.

He pulled her tunic over her head, and his heart sank at the binding encircling her breasts. "Ye've had this on the whole time?"

She nodded, her cheeks tinging pink in embarrassment.

He reached behind her and started to unwind the cloth, and was soon blessed with the milky globes of her breasts and her sigh of relief. He bent his head and kissed each rose-colored nipple.

She gasped and shivered.

"Dinna ever hide these from me again," he said and licked first her left breast, circling his tongue around the nipple before drawing it into his mouth, teasing it into a taut peak. Then he moved onto the right breast and did the same.

"Colin," she whispered.

He smiled against her breast. It was the first time he'd heard her speak his name in such a manner, and he wanted to hear it again.

He hooked his fingers in the waist of her trews and drew them down her legs. Her porcelain skin was revealed inch by inch the further he went.

He pulled off her boots and quickly got rid of her stockings before pulling her trews off her legs completely.

She lay on the bed naked before him and his breath caught in his throat.

"Ye're so beautiful."

She moved her arms to shield her body from his eyes, but he pulled her hands away.

"Dinna," he whispered. "Ye should never feel the need to hide yerself from me."

Seonag sighed. "I've never..." She looked away shyly, letting her voice trail off without finishing her statement.

But Colin knew what she was telling him, even without saying the words.

Her cheeks colored with embarrassment.

His fingers feathered lightly over her arms and he watched as the golden hairs stood on end and her skin raised into gooseflesh at his touch.

She'd been through a lot. She should be resting and coming down from the excitement of everything that had transpired in the past day. Seonag didn't need him adding this pressure to her on top of everything else.

Colin lifted her and pulled the throw she was laying out from under her and laid her back down, covering her.

She looked up at him, confusion clouding her face.

"What are ye doing?"

"Ye should rest. It doesna feel 'tis the right time."

"Ye dinna want me?" Her voice was quiet when she asked him.

Colin shook his head. "Nay, lass. Quite the opposite 'tis true. I wasna lying when I spoke before. I want ye. I've wanted ye. But the timing needs to be right."

She sat up, grasping the throw and using it to cover her breasts. Hurt darkened her delicate features.

"I spoke the truth as well. These feelings. The flutter deep in my belly when ye're near. No one has ever made me feel this way." She let the blanket fall away, revealing herself to him once again, and crawled over to where he sat on the corner of the bed.

That move was the most tantalizing thing he'd ever seen. Her strong-willed demeanor making her his perfect match.

She turned her face into his and captured his lips. This time, her tongue entered his mouth, taking the lead. His pulse quickened, excited from Seonag taking the initiative.

She broke the kiss. "I want this. I want ye, Colin."

"There's no going back, lass," he whispered. "I'll be forever yers." And he meant every word.

"I dinna want to go back. Make me yers, Colin Harris."

Colin's body thrummed with new feelings he'd never experienced before. Seonag was doing this to him.

"Do ye ken what ye are doing to me, lass?"

She trailed a slender finger down his chest, and even

through his tunic, the gesture seared into his skin. He caught her fingers and kissed the tips, one by one.

"The same ye are doing to me, I fear."

"Ye've nothing to fear from me. Ever."

"I know."

"I willna leave the sea," he confessed.

She smiled. "Me either. Much to my mother's chagrin."

He growled deep in his throat and nipped at her neck. "We'll rule the sea, side by side."

"Aye," she agreed. "But on my father's ship. The *Revenge of Hades* deserves to be captained by someone who has a vested interest in her. I think Da would be happy to know that it was us taking her helm." She blessed him with a dazzling smile and all thoughts but Seonag left his head.

She wrapped her hands around his neck and brought him down with her to settle on the mattress. She kissed him fully. Deeply.

A moan escaped her lips and he reveled at the sound. It was sweet music to his ears.

He kissed the skin of her shoulder and she hissed. He smiled against her flesh, anticipating the pleasure they both would soon be lost in.

Laying back, Seonag concentrated on Colin's gentle touch. His warm hands heated her skin wherever he touched and she didn't want him to stop.

His fingers brushed the nestle of curls at her apex and she hissed. The feeling unlike anything she'd ever felt before and she wanted it to continue.

Colin pushed a finger into her soft folds, and she couldn't stop the moan that burst forth, but Colin swallowed it with a kiss.

He moved slow and gentle, taking care not to hurt her as he worked his finger in and out of her velvety entrance as she moaned. Her breath hitched with each stroke.

She'd never been with a man before. And she was impressed with the gentleness Colin was showing her.

He nuzzled her neck, sending shivers down her spine, as he worked her with first one finger, and then another, readying her for him.

"If ye want me to stop, lass, say so now."

He was sincere. Seonag knew if she told him to stop, he would. But she didn't want him to. She wanted him. All of him.

"If we go much further, I willna be able to stop."

"I dinna want ye to."

That was all the urging he needed. She watched as he broke their contact, leaving her skin cool from their lack of touch as he leaned back on his knees and made quick work of his tunic, boots and finally his trews. His manhood bounced, hard and long. Ready.

Seonag couldn't help but widen her eyes as she noticed his size. She began to shiver, in both anticipation and a bit of fear. She knew what was coming would be painful at first. But she also knew Colin would be as gentle as possible.

Colin sank back into her arms and kissed her neck, his fingers entering her wet folds again, getting her ready to take him.

He stroked her long and deep until she was writhing and bucking beneath him. He positioned himself over her and settled between her legs. He captured her mouth in his and she felt his manhood bump against her opening.

"Ready?" Colin asked.

She bit her bottom lip, worry making her hesitate.

Colin had the patience of a saint as he waited for her consent.

She lifted her head and placed a kiss on his lips and whispered, "I'm ready."

She felt him nudge her opening, and she widened her eyes at the feeling of pressure.

He pushed forward slowly, entering her and paused when he hit the barrier of her maidenhead.

Seonag gasped.

"Shh, try to relax. Do ye trust me?"

She searched his face and found nothing but concern. He was being so kind and she appreciated his patience with her.

She nodded, urging him on with a wary smile.

He captured her lips again and thrust his tongue into her mouth at the same time he reared his hips back and plunged forward, forcing his way past her maidenhead.

Seonag's cry of pain was swallowed by Colin's deep kiss, and he stilled his hips, allowing her to grow accustomed to him.

After several moments, the pain began to ebb and she began to shift under him.

Colin took that as a sign to continue on. He gently rocked his hips in small movements. Concern creasing his forehead as he slowly withdrew and entered again, his strokes long and slow.

She couldn't help the tear that escaped her eye. She wasn't in pain any longer and the sensation that replaced it was borderline pleasant. The feeling getting better with each stroke from Colin.

Colin kissed it away as it started to trail down her cheek.

"I'm so sorry. Dinna cry. Ye feel so good, lass," Colin cooed. "Come with me, Seonag. Let me take ye over the edge."

He quickened his pace and her body began to thrum. A vibration starting deep in her core, growing, and building until it couldn't be contained any longer."

"That's it, lass. Let it go."

"Colin!" Seonag cried out into the room, her voice echoing off the walls. Her limbs took on a life of their own. Contracting and pulsating as her release overtook her.

With a final thrust, Colin grunted his own release. His growl was almost louder than hers.

Both of them panted heavily, their breaths coming out in loud huffs.

Colin rolled off her, but took her with him, so she lay upon his chest.

She listened to the steady staccato of his heartbeat. She could feel the thumping against her cheek.

He placed a soft kiss on her forehead. "I hope I didna hurt ye too bad, lass."

She shook her head against his chest, "Ye didna."

"Good. The first time is always the worst." He stroked the smooth skin of her back. Then reached over and pulled the throw over them. "Sleep now. We'll talk more in the morn."

"Colin?"

"Hmm?"

"I love ye. I'm sorry that I lied."

"Och, lass. I love ye, too. All is forgiven. If ye hadn't lied, ye'd never have been on my ship, and we would cease to be." He stroked her back. "All is as it should be."

She sighed, content in Colin's arms. Never in all of her life had she ever thought that fateful night at the inn would lead her to this moment.

Seonag stayed awake for a while, listening to Colin's breathing. A sound she'd grown accustomed to for the past few weeks, but this night, it seemed so much more special.

EPILOGUE

*O*ne month later

Seonag and Colin sat on a pine bench across from Margaret, in the small house Seonag used to share with her mother, scarcely able to contain their huge grins at the surprise they had for her.

They'd been away this past month, refilling the ship's supplies after taking down Storm and his crew, then sailing home.

Margaret sighed from her rocking chair, a gift from her late husband. He'd made it himself and even carved the design of his flag into the wood. "After being the wife of a pirate, Seonag, I canna say that I'm overly happy at yer decision to stay with Colin." She looked at Colin. "No offense, Captain."

"None taken, ma'am. I understand. Yer daughter's best interests are first and foremost in yer mind. I can assure ye that they are mine as well." Colin clasped Seonag's hand, his thumb stroking her palm, shooting a thrill up her arm.

"Ma, I know yer concern. Colin is a good man." She patted his knee and squeezed. "He's put up with me and forgave my deception once he understood the reason behind it. Storm has been dealt with, and the *Revenge of Hades* is being repaired as we speak." The repair was no small task. The ship was heavily damaged in the attack, but Colin was committed to restoring the vessel to its former sailing glory. "When next she sets sail, she'll have a faithful crew with a deserving captain at the helm."

And she would. After weeks of discussion, Colin decided to gift Peggy the *Hella*. The man was more than capable of running his own ship and crew. He'd been practically doing that all along for the *Hella,* so it only made sense that he continue to do so.

Which meant that Colin and Seonag would helm the *Revenge of Hades*, carrying on her father's legacy.

Seonag knew Colin would miss Peggy, but Derrick had proven to be more than capable. So Colin was going to train him for the position of quartermaster.

"And ye know I've always been happier in the water than on land," Seonag continued.

"'Tis true," Margaret conceded. "But 'tis still a danger. And a lass at sea? Who's ever heard of such a thing?"

"I'll be in good hands, Ma."

Margaret looked at Colin, and Seonag knew her mother saw the same thing that she did. A strong, confident man that would give his life for her if it came to it.

Her mother nodded and threw up her hands. "Fine! Ye have my blessing. But, if I hear anything of ill will against my daughter, I will come and hunt ye down myself, Colin Harris."

Colin belted out a laugh. "I would expect nothing less." He smiled warmly. "Now for our surprise." He clasped his hands together and rubbed them in anticipation before standing up and walking to the thick oak door.

He opened it, bent to pick something up, and then turned

back into the house, ducking slightly so as not to bang his head on the low doorframe and nudging the door shut with his boot.

"This, my lady, is for ye." He put the small wooden chest down on the table. "A gift from Sean. Yer husband was a fine man that loved his family and wanted nothing more than ye to be happy and cared for." He opened the silver clasp and lifted the lid of the chest, revealing the gold coin inside. "This is the least I could do to make it right."

Margaret gasped, covering her face with her hands as tears sprouted in her eyes.

Seonag watched as her mother embraced Colin, the sadness of losing her father lifting just a little.

Colin smiled at Seonag as her mother held on to him, and she knew from that point on, she never wanted to be away from his side.

They'd rule the sea from the *Revenge of Hades*, side by side.

The future was theirs, and she couldn't wait to see what it held.

A PIRATE'S TREASURE

SCOTTISH ROGUES OF THE HIGH SEAS, BOOK 1

What happens when a mercenary gets more than he bargains for?

Pirate mercenary Lochlan MacLean loves his life on the sea, yet yearns for lands of his own to call home. He chooses his missions wisely, taking care they don't go against his strict moral code. But when a deceitful father hires him for a challenging task - kidnapping a woman - he questions himself and his ethics. The spoils in both land and coin will fulfill his dream, and he can't resist the job or the beautiful lass.

Strong-willed Lady Isobel Willys has always been promised her future is hers to choose until her father betrays her by promising her to a widowed Scottish laird under the guise of a peace treaty between their borderland families. While journeying to visit family, her travel party is set upon by a handsome highlander who she believes is her betrothed too impatient to wait. Soon she finds out everything she's ever known is a lie and her family's future is uncertain.

Isobel's fierce attraction to Lochlan threatens the promised peace for her family. She must make a choice: go against her family's wishes to live the life she chooses, or lose the man she might be in love with. Lochlan's desire for Isobel could cost him lands and coin. Can he give up the one thing he's always wanted for the one thing he never knew he needed?

Order A Pirate's Treasure now: https://amzn.to/3wzMOFV

Scan the code to be taken directly to the purchase link.

ALSO BY BRENNA ASH

Historical Romance
Scottish Rogues of the High Seas Series
A Pirate's Treasure

∾

Contemporary Romance
Second Chances

∾

Paranormal Romance
A Kiss of Stone

ABOUT THE AUTHOR

Brenna Ash is addicted to coffee and chocolate. When she's not writing, she can be found either poolside reading a book, or in front of the TV, binge-watching her favorite shows, *Outlander* and *Sons of Anarchy*. She lives in Florida with her husband and a very, very spoiled cat named Lilly. She loves to interact with her readers on social media. Please feel free to follow her at the following platforms:

www.facebook.com/BrennaAshAuthor
www.twitter.com/brenna_ash
www.pinterest.com/brenna1168
www.instagram.com/BrennaAshAuthor

To stay up to date on all things Brenna Ash, including book news, release dates and contest info, please sign-up for her newsletter on her website.

www.BrennaAsh.com